MW01479378

SALAD DAYS

by Claire Rothman

SALAD DAYS

short stories
by Claire Rothman

Cormorant Books

Copyright © Claire Rothman, 1990

Second Printing, May, 1991

Published with the assistance of The Canada Council and the Ontario Arts Council.

The author would like to acknowledge the following magazines and periodicals where some of this material has appeared: *Fiddlehead* (Winter/89), *Canadian Woman's Studies* (Summer/90 and Spring/88) and *The New Canadian Review* (Spring/87).

Cover from a watercolour on paper, *Red Dahlias at Night,* by Carol H. Fraser, courtesy of the artist and The Canada Council Art Bank.

Published by Cormorant Books, RR 1, Dunvegan, Ontario, Canada K0C 1J0

Printed and bound in Canada.

Canadian Cataloguing in Publication Data

  Rothman, Claire, 1958-
       Salad days

ISBN 0-920953-27-1

    I. Title.

PS8585.O8435S24 1990   C813'.54   C90-090148-9
PR9199.3.R68S24 1990

To Ann with love

Table of Contents

Enough, 7
August, 20
Beyond The Pale, 40
Salad Days, 54
Wing-beat, 72
This Really Isn't It, 84
Jyoti, 97
Xanadu, 108
Remembering the Dead, 121
Prosperity, 127

Enough

The man had slept there again last night. The little boy could always tell because his mother shut the bedroom door when the man slept with her. Before he started sleeping there, it was left open. The boy liked it that way, his door and his mother's wide open so that the same air, the same sounds, the same smells could pass through both their rooms. He could call to her or sing in his bed, and know that she would hear him. The man had slept in their apartment for so many nights that the little boy had a hard time remembering what it had been like without him.

His mother's bed was flat and very low, mounted on a platform raised slightly from the floor. The little boy stood at the foot of it gazing down at a sky blue quilt and at two sleeping figures. His mother was curled up like a cat in one corner. Her hair flowed out along the pillow slip in a long, rust-coloured tangle, half obscuring her face, which was pale and lightly freckled. The man called Ray lay on his back, his arms and legs flung out, forming ridges and gullies deep in the quilt. He breathed heavily, rhythmically, through a mouth that was slack and pulled down slightly at the edges. The little boy moved closer to his mother and stared through the hair to the half-hidden face. She stirred and opened her eyes.

"It's early to come visiting," she said and reached out

to stroke his head. "What's up, Baby Blue?"

He wasn't a baby. His mother called him this even though his real name was Jacob. She lifted the quilt so it looked like the entrance to a dark cave, and he dove in. The smell of sleep and bodies was strong as he climbed over her and slid down the skin of her back into the bed's warm middle. He kicked his legs in the air, making the quilt rise up like a giant tent. It hovered above their bodies for an instant and then fell, graceful as a sigh.

The man groaned and turned his head away when he saw the boy. "Christ," he said. "You should train him not to do that." His voice was low and full of sleep. "It gives me the creeps having him in here, staring. He's old enough to understand."

Jacob lay perfectly still. He heard the man roll over and found himself on the floor again, his pyjama top dishevelled and twisted by the man's big hands.

"Go on," said the man, pushing him towards the door. "Go and play." It was a hard push, and it propelled Jacob forward across the floor. His feet made a light padding sound against the wood as he fled. He walked quickly, not daring to look back, imagining the man rising up out of the bed, towering higher and higher until his head grazed the ceiling, following him down the shadowy corridor.

Jacob's room was full of light. The thin ricepaper blind covering his window didn't block out the morning; it let light filter in, diffusing it and splashing it on each wall. Jacob knelt down on the cool wood floor and pulled a drawer out from his clothes chest. His mother had said that because he was four he must put on his own socks.

He didn't want his breakfast. His mother was up now and had prepared his favourite thing, and still he wouldn't eat.

Instead he watched bits of green marshmallow, cut into the shape of four-leaf clovers, float in circles on the surface of the milk. The rest of his meal had sunk to the bottom of the bowl where it lay, soggy and inedible. He cupped his spoon over the marshmallow bits, trying to submerge them.

His mother left the room. Jacob had put her out of his mind when her voice came floating down the hall. It was a voice she used when she was angry. He could picture her, standing in her half-opened bathrobe, her hair all out of order and flying about her face. Her fists would be clenched tight and her eyes too, as if she wanted to shut the world out. She was yelling. A torrent of words, ugly, shrill things, was pouring through the apartment, like pins from her sewing box when he upset it. He hated her like this. The man was making noise too. He was shouting and things were falling and breaking. The boy kept trying to push down the green bits in his bowl. He pushed more and more recklessly, sending waves of milk up over the rim. Then, without understanding why, he swiped at it with his forearm sending it sliding along the milk-slippery table top and crashing onto the floor. It broke into sharp wedges, littering the kitchen with ceramic, and bits of soggy brown food.

The voices had stopped. His mother was crying now. She was moaning and every once in a while she screamed out in a wild, disturbing way. Jacob heard footsteps start down the corridor. They were too heavy, too widely spaced to be his mother's, and the floors trembled and shook. It was the man. He had heard the crash, he knew somehow that the bowl was broken, and who the culprit was. Jacob slipped down from his chair to the floor. He crouched there, shivering, staring at a crack where dirt was forcing the tile to curl up and in on itself. Cracks worried him. It was possible that dark things lived under there and if he pried the tile loose, beetles would stare out at him. The steps came closer. Jacob clasped his knees tightly. He felt his insides shudder and heave, and then rush out, slippery, uncontrolled.

The steps passed the kitchen and receded down the hall to the front door. It slammed. For a long time Jacob didn't move. He just crouched, shivering and staring at the dirt-lined crack with eyes that would not see.

His mother was being nice. He was in the bathtub now, with his red boat and a plastic banana that floated. His mother was taking the banana and rubbing it over his stomach, pretending it was eating him up. "Mmm," she said. "Baby Blue's tender tummy. Mmmmm." She did not mind the mess. Did not say a word about the cereal or about his body covered with smelly dirt. She had picked him up, carried him to the bathroom, run a steaming, big bath, and begun to play. She did not look playful. Her lip was swollen and a cut with blood caked at its edges stared out from one of her cheeks. But still, she was being nice, and her voice was low and calm. He didn't like the washcloth. It was rough and prickly and scratched him. When his mother tried to wash him he squirmed away, clutching his toys to his chest.

Outside, the cold made his skin feel parched and stretched. His mother had brought him to the little park across from their building, and asked some children to keep an eye on him. The children nodded solemnly, but as soon as she turned her back, they ran off down the street in a furious game of chase. Still, the park wasn't empty. The two girls and their sitter were there, as they often were in the morning. The big one was on top of the monkey bars watching him, letting her body hang upside down and swing. She was very strong and could flip over the bar with straight arms, and do tricks. The little one, who was just slightly older than Jacob, was very serious. She liked digging in the sand. But it was Genevieve whom Jacob liked most of all. She looked after them. She was reading a magazine on a bench in the sun. Her shoes lay abandoned by the sandbox, stuffed with red wool socks, and she stretched her toes in the yellowish dirt beneath the bench. Jacob walked over to the sandbox. The little girl was building a wall around some mounds that he supposed were huts.

Genevieve looked up from her pages and saw him. She called out his name and some other things he couldn't understand. He loved it when she spoke. It was almost like singing, the way her voice rose and fell and the words blended one into the next.

The little girl let him have one of her shovels. He was helping with the wall, scooping the damp sand that lay just beneath the surface and patting it into a solid, connecting hump. The sides of his palms were black and gritty and his hands were cold, but he didn't mind because the village was huge and growing more beautiful. He had been crouching beside the girl for a long time and his legs were hurting. He stood up, holding the shovel, and rubbed an arm over his eyes. Grains of sand from the shovel rained down on him, falling in his face and he stumbled backwards, demolishing part of the wall that he himself had just finished and crushing a tower with a toothpick flag. The little girl flew at him and pushed him back off the wall. A torrent of words came from her lips, words that leapt and flowed like Genevieve's, but faster and shriller because she was angry and close to tears. She snatched the shovel away and left him in the cool sand where he had fallen, his hands stiffly out in front of him as if they still held it. He opened his mouth wide, stunned with outrage and shock, and bellowed like an infant.

Genevieve's feet were beside him on the grass, rubbing each other, twitching in their concern. She knelt down so that her knees cradled his shoulders and cooed with her strange, calming words. She addressed the girl, who was standing not far off, pouting at the sand. A second explosion of words came from the child. "I hate him," she said, this time in English so he would understand. "He's dumb! He broke a wall." Genevieve listened and rocked him gently. His wails had subsided into fierce hiccups which jerked his body, and his nose was running badly.

"*Assez!*" she said to the little girl, and from her tone Jacob knew that the little girl was wrong and mean, and that he might get the shovel back. The little girl pouted but didn't dare talk back to Genevieve. Eventually, on Genevieve's orders, she offered him his shovel.

Genevieve dug deep into the pocket of her jeans and pulled out a package of candies. "Wine jellies!" the little girl called, and her voice sailed across the park with its wonderful news. The older sister flipped down off her bar and came running. Genevieve gave three jellies to each of them. Jacob's were purple and the translucent green of peeled grapes. They glistened in his gritty palm and looked almost too perfect to eat.

Genevieve bent over him and whispered in his ear. Her breath was moist and pleasantly sour, and to Jacob, her words were like the jellies themselves, exquisite, mouthwatering, comforting.

"Assez, assez," Jacob said, smiling at his mother as she ladled soup into a bowl for his supper. He made all sorts of other noises too, rushing melodious sounds like Genevieve made for him in the park.

"That's French," his mother said, looking at him intently. Jacob began a song of made-up words that had the same comforting ebb and flow.

"We don't need a serenade," the man said.

Jacob's mother was standing by the man's chair and he stroked the back of her legs. Jacob kept humming, but silently, in his head. His cheeks were flushed and he could feel blood pulsing in steady, hot beats against the inside of his skull. His mother asked him if he wanted more and he didn't look up. He slipped under the table with crayons and some paper while his mother prepared dinner for the man. She was talking and her voice mixed with the man's, and the words slowly became vaguer and less distinct. It felt almost pleasant there, under the table, with the low backdrop of noise.

Later on he heard them laughing in the bedroom. The door was shut, but still he could hear her teasing the man, maybe telling him riddles, and laughing in that happy, breathy way she had. He went to sleep with this light sound in his ears and dreamt that she was leaning over him in the crib he'd slept in as a baby. She was leaning over the bars, laughing with him, loving him.

In the morning the man whistled in the bathroom. He was shaving before he went to his office. They sat around the table and watched him eat a stack of toast. Jacob liked the way he spread the butter thickly on each piece so it soaked completely through. Pools of melted grease spotted his plate. After the butter he spooned on great amounts of cherry jam and ate the whole thing fast, before any of it oozed away. Jacob watched in awe. His mother always spread his thin. It looked meagre and uninteresting beside what the man called Ray was eating.

"Hey, kiddo!" Ray said through a mouthful of jam. He wiped his fingers and his golden moustache with the tip of a paper towel. "Got something for you." He reached up on top of the refrigerator and pulled down a red and blue baseball cap. "It's the Expos, kid. It's a lucky hat."

"It's really nice, Ray," his mother said, admiring it in Ray's hands. "What do you say, Baby Blue?"

Jacob looked out the kitchen window. The tree in their front yard had burst into brilliant amber, the colour of the pumpkins they would gut for Hallowe'en.

"C'mon kiddo," the man said. He squatted down, hooked his fingers through Jacob's beltloops, and pulled him between his knees. "It's a peace offering," he said. "Don't be so hard on an old man."

Jacob stared at the floor. His arms and legs were limp and shivery. The crack between the tiles was still there, gaping like a dark smile at his feet. All the rest of the tiles were perfect. They had a black centre and white bars that fanned out like the blades of a propeller. When he stared too long, his eyes went swimmy and bars began to spin and whirl on the flat surface of the floor.

Ray's voice came across a great distance. It was as if he were standing on a wide open plain, and Ray was a tiny speck on the horizon. He felt dizzy thinking of the man and his mother so far away. Something landed heavily on his head. He put his hands up, as if he were shielding himself from a blow, and felt the stiff nylon meshing and the plastic rim. Ray relaxed his hold of the beltloops and Jacob slumped backwards against a chair.

In the park he sat alone in the spot where Genevieve usually sunned. A woman stood on the grass with a baby who was just learning to walk. She held out her hands and the child staggered towards her. He looked so clumsy and small, Jacob wanted to laugh. Jacob removed the baseball cap from his head. He got on his hands and knees and began to scrape the sand with it. It was like a trowel, new and stiff enough that it gathered the grains of sand quite easily. He filled it full and then dropped it, bottom side up. Some of the sand spilled out and he scooped it back in with his hands. He pushed more sand on top and then patted sand walls up near the cap's sides. Soon the entire thing was covered. The only telltale sign was a small dune rising up in a shaded corner of the sandbox.

Jacob walked on the grass around the sandbox, contemplating the dune. He reached his cold soiled hands into his pants pockets and discovered jelly candies, forgotten and left over from yesterday. There were two of them, lime green, and he popped them both into his mouth at once. Sand was embedded in their sugary skins and when Jacob chewed it was as if cannons fired inside him. Each time his teeth closed on the sweet green meat, his head was filled with roaring explosions.

When he looked up from the sand, his mother was running across the grass towards him. Jacob was confused and thought that she had heard him all the way across the street, up in their apartment. She would be angry and tell him loudly, so the other woman would hear, that eating dirt was for babies, not for grown-up boys of four years old. But when she reached the sandbox she did not pry open his mouth. She did not even ask to see what he was chewing on.

"Where are the other kids?" she asked, wetting her handkerchief with spittle and wiping his face and hands. "They were supposed to bring you home half an hour ago. You could have come yourself. Aren't you hungry for your lunch?"

Jacob hung his head. He let her drag him across the park, down the street to their building, and up the stairs.

"You're one hell of a kid," she said, pulling off his billie boots outside their door. "One hell of a glum, mysterious kid."

In the afternoon his mother shut herself in the livingroom with a typewriter. The clicking of the machine and its periodic ring irritated him, and he couldn't concentrate on his toys. His mother didn't look up when he walked out the door and into the corridor of the building. He decided to visit Mr Mahoney down the hall. Mr Mahoney was an old man. He stayed in his room all day watching television, and at night, ladies came with food to fix him supper. The apartment was very stuffy and dark and filled with a sweet, medicinal smell. It wasn't a bad smell, just one that made Jacob dozy and apt to fall asleep. He slipped inside the door, which was unlatched for emergencies.

"Well, well," said Mr Mahoney. "Look at what the cat brought in."

There was no cat. Mr Mahoney always said this when Jacob came for a visit. It was his way of saying hello. He nodded from the sofa where he was watching a football game. Jacob lay down on his stomach in the middle of the rug. Usually he didn't have too much to say to the old man, and sometimes he was so quiet that Mr Mahoney forgot all about him and took a nap. He lay like this for a while, watching the little men run back and forth across the screen. Every once in a while Mr Mahoney would rise up a little ways off the couch and shoot his fist into the air. He laughed and called out, "Ooh Nellie" or "That'll fix 'em good." He was not talking to Jacob when he said these things. He didn't look towards the rug. He was just trying the words out, it seemed, for the pleasure of making a noise. Jacob understood this. *Ooh Nellie* must feel nice curling off your tongue, especially if you lingered and stretched it out the way Mr Mahoney did.

Jacob went to Mr Mahoney's kitchen and opened the low cupboard door. He knew exactly where to look; Mr Mahoney had shown him the place. He took out the large square tin box and began to pry off the top. Inside were cookies. They weren't his favourites. They didn't have cream fillings or sugar coatings. Mr Mahoney had simple tastes. He liked oatmeal, and something he called *fly biscuits* with squashed black raisins that looked like house flies. Jacob took a handful of oatmeal ones, with enough for Mr Mahoney, and went back to the television room.

His mother was standing beside the sofa. "Jacob," she said when she saw him, "you will be the death of me." Her hair was half fallen as if she'd been running. "He's so damn quiet," she was saying to Mr Mahoney. "Never tells me he's wandering off. I go mad with worry." She bent over Jacob, whose fists were closed and full of cookies. "You must never, never sneak off like that again. Are you listening Jacob?" Her words fell about him like slivers of glass. "Why do you do it?" She squeezed his shoulders and shook him. Jacob said nothing. He poked his running shoe into Mr Mahoney's rug. His mother spoke for a while longer to Mr Mahoney who was sitting straight up on the couch, drinking in the drama in his livingroom. He almost never received visitors in the afternoons, so this was an occasion. Then, without giving Jacob a chance to say goodbye, Jacob's mother took his arm and dragged him back towards their apartment. He couldn't keep a grip on all the cookies as she pulled him, and scattered a line of crumbs, like Gretel, all the way down the corridor, from Mr Mahoney's door to theirs.

That night, the man came in early. He was wearing jeans, just like Jacob was, and while they sat in the kitchen, he kept throwing a can of chili into the air and catching it with one hand. The can made a pleasant slapping sound against his palm. He came over to where Jacob and his mother were sitting and passed his hand over the top of Jacob's head. "Hey, pardner," he said, "where's the hat?"

Jacob didn't like the weight of the man's hand. He went limp in his mother's arms and slid out of reach down to the kitchen floor.

"It's weird the way he goes all soft and quiet," the man said. He knelt down in front of the little boy and shook him gently. "C'mon Jacob. Where is it?"

Jacob could hardly hear him. He kept his eyes low, staring at the floor. His stomach began to cramp and make ugly, frightened noises.

"Talk to me, Jacob. You lose it or something?" The man's hands loosened and Jacob slumped lower on the floor. "Christ!" the man said. He stood up and began to toss the can from one hand to the other. "I give up. That kid of yours is weird, Gill."

"I'd like to know," he said, pulling open drawers and slamming them shut again, "just where the hell the can opener's got to."

His mother, who until then had watched quietly, perched on a tall wicker bar stool by the counter, made a worried, fluttering motion. "Forget the chili," she said. "Can't you see there's something wrong!" Her hands waved back and forth, like the wings of a bird, and she hurried her words as if she didn't believe the man would listen. "He's terrified, Ray. You scare the wits right out of him."

The man had a funny, pained look on his face. "Don't start coming after me for all the kid's problems," he said. "I'm not the goddamn *father*." Then he spoke more gently. "Maybe it's just a stage he's passing through."

But she was shaking her head, shutting her eyes tight the way she did when she was very upset. "It's not a stage," she said, her voice defiant and straining against tears. "God, this is too awful."

The man put the unopened can of chili down on the counter. Then, without looking at either of them, he went out to the hall for his jacket. The door slammed hard, shaking the walls of the apartment.

Jacob's mother squatted on the floor, collapsing over him as if the strength had been wrung out of her. She was crying and her tears fell forward over his body making tiny, slapping noises against the black and white tiles. He squirmed around in her arms. Lines of black dripped from her eyes and she wept loudly, as if she didn't feel him there.

"Assez," he said faintly, and stroked her hair. He said other things, mimicking the soothing tones and sounds of Genevieve, and thought of jelly candies, sour, dusted in sugar, gem-coloured, like the ones she gave him in the park.

His mother looked up, her eyes swimming with tears, the skin of her cheeks smudged with grey. She wiped her face, and suddenly began to laugh. "You're right," she said, "assez," but she started to cry again.

"Assez, assez," she said, her entire body shaking in his startled, childish arms.

August

The summer I turned fourteen was particularly wet and grey. I stayed at home after school closed, staring at the world through rain-streaked windows, working my way through piles of romance magazines. My mother couldn't pass the livingroom without making some comment. She said I won the sweepstakes for laziness. Lists of chores hung on the refrigerator door in her neat hand. She had high hopes. But it was all I could do to rouse myself from the couch and wander down the hall to my room for nail lacquer, or to replenish the magazine supply. I had no energy for anything.

  I was the eldest of five girls. My sisters still went to day camp. I had outgrown this but was too young to get a summer job. There was nothing to do but lounge. My mother called it an "in between" age. I wasn't like my sisters any longer, but I wasn't an adult either. She reminded me of that often enough. I had to be inside the house by nine thirty every night. There was nowhere in particular I wanted to go, but it was humiliating all the same. My sisters got to play outside till dusk, which in the month of June fell just about that hour. If I came in late I lost my allowance just like them. It robbed me of my dignity.

  Montreal had turned into a ghost town. My friends had left for cottages or overnight camps where they practiced riding and tennis. I wished I could leave home like them, but with five children in the family it was out of the question. I felt martyred for my baby sisters and moped all the more at life's injustice. Some days I roused myself and walked over to the park. There were tennis courts there and the attendant, a boy named Arthur, was older than me and very good looking. He'd been elected King during carnival week at my school. I used to wait for someone to lob a ball over the fence and run to retrieve it. Sometimes Arthur even nodded in my direction, and struck up a conversation. But the courts were flooded every second day and closed down most of the time. Arthur hid out in the men's room or else gave up and went home. In the end, the park proved as lifeless and dull as anywhere else. I was forced back to the livingroom, to my magazines and daydreams.

After six weeks of this, my mother finally lost her cool. She kept up a stream of activity, not even breaking pace on the hottest days. Watching her depleted me. She aired blankets on the back verandah, washed the walls and floors, did laundry, cooking, packed four bag lunches every morning for my siblings. The sight of me stretched out on her couch, the floor littered with paper, a bowl of popcorn at my elbow, set her off. It was as if a horsefly got her. She literally went red with rage. One night at the end of July she telephoned her parents. They lived in Toronto, but were vacationing on a muddy lake somewhere in southern Ontario.

My mother had spent summers there as a child. It was called Bramlea and she always spoke of it as if it were special, a place of real beauty. I'd seen it once on one of my father's summer vacations. We'd all driven down, an endless trip during which my sisters vomited one after the other, each spurring on the next, all over the back seat. I remember trying not to breathe for three hundred miles. It was the last long voyage by automobile my father ever took with us.

When we arrived we were desperate for water. We spilled out of the car, stripping off shorts and shirts as we went, littering the path down to the dock. We'd already fished the bathing suits out of our suitcases and changed in the car's back seat (coyly, beneath beach towels). Being the eldest with the longest legs, I was the first one at the dock. I peered in and set the tone for the whole visit by refusing to climb down the ladder. Weeds covered the lake bottom like a carpet. They waved, slick, hairlike, rippling the water's surface. At night we spread sleeping bags on the livingroom floor because there weren't enough beds. My grandmother, who for some reason went by the nickname Petes (her real name was Gloria), told us not to whisper or we'd wake up the mice.

My mother wanted me to go back there. I'd stay the month of August, she said. It'd do me good.

I arrived at the bus depot at Bramlea just as the sun was sinking. It had been hazy and uncertain all afternoon and with darkness coming the sky turned a strange greyish yellow. Rain had followed me, my grandfather was later to observe, across the border and all the way from Montreal. That summer, I began calling my grandfather by his real name, Harry. Before, I used to call him Grampa Harold, but when I got off the bus that night I felt pretty grown up. I'd travelled over three hundred miles on my own, and I figured I had a right. All the way to Toronto I'd sat with a woman who'd just gone through a divorce. She told me the details. How she'd raised kids. How he was a drinker. How he had his little affairs, and gradually the marriage eroded. "We were like ships passing in the night. I barely knew him at the end." When she said goodbye to me at the Toronto station she got all sentimental. She didn't know anything about me (she'd done all the talking), but she said I was smart, and "mature beyond your years."

So when I got off the bus I called out, "Hi, Harry." I said it simply, looking him in the eye as if it were the most natural thing in the world. It's amazing what you can get away with when you look people in the eye. I was trying on a hat. He could have knocked it off my head, sent it flying, told me it wasn't my place, but he just laughed and hugged me as if I'd been using it for years.

Harry loved to work. He'd grown up on a farm where everyone was expected to pull his weight. If he was ever caught idling he once told me, his father or an older brother would take a leather thong down from the wall and remind him of all the chores that needed doing. You'd have thought he'd grow up hating work, but he was just the opposite. He abhorred idleness. There was a hammock on his lawn strung between a birch tree and the porch, but neither he nor Petes used it. It was there for show. A functionless emblem of summer. Harry couldn't sit, let alone lie, in one place for more than a few minutes. Like my mother he dreamt up an endless series of tasks and set about doing them in a resolute way. Unlike her, he was always cheerful about it. It was the thing he liked most and he was impatient when darkness fell and he was forced to rest.

The night I arrived, rain came down harder over Bramlea than it had all summer. I was in my jeans sipping cocoa (the real kind, made with honey and milk) when Petes disappeared. It was still light outside, barely nine o'clock, and I figured she'd gone to get a book or something. A few minutes later she came out of the bedroom in a ratty mustard-coloured bathrobe.

She had flannel on underneath, I could see the collar, and her face was slathered with white cream. She kissed me lightly and said she was retiring. She pecked Harry's cheek as well. He slept in a different room. I'd known this from when I visited them in Toronto, but I'd never thought much about it. Now it made me wonder. Poor old Harry, banished to a separate room, and what was more, Petes didn't look all that appealing after dark. In Montreal my parents shared a bed. They were private about sex, and frankly I still don't know when they did it (I have no recollections of ever walking in on them), but at least the bed was there. A symbol brimming with adult mystery. I went to sleep wondering about Petes and Harry. Trying to picture them young.

I awoke to smells of frying bacon and toast. Rain was pummelling the roof. I dozed while Harry and Petes got agitated, wondering whether to knock and wake me or let me eat my breakfast cold. Finally I got up and Petes sat with me, watching me crumble dried-out pork into small bits and dissolve them on my tongue. Harry stuck his head in from the porch as I was finishing. The rain had stopped, he said. It was time to fix the road.

I was still in my pyjamas. By the time I changed into shorts and a T-shirt he was half way up the road that linked his cottage to the highway. This road was dirt, about a kilometre in length, and rose in periodic, gentle hills. My grandfather was wearing stained work pants. He carried an old bucket full of sand and two spades. I fell into step beside him and he explained what we would do with the pleasure of someone proposing a set of tennis, a boatride on the lake.

"This sand will do the trick. The rain really cut up the road's surface."

Harry didn't own the road. It was a public access and

other cottagers and farmers used it. But Harry didn't think in terms of who owned what. It needed to be done and he had the time. It wasn't hard work, he said, and in the long run, life would be better for everyone. It struck me as pretty left wing. Harry had voted conservative every election since the First World War. In theory, he was all for the free market. In practice, however, he was something between a socialist and a saint. He was always weighing things with an eye to the common good. I admired Harry's zeal but at the same time I found it peculiar. It was just about as foreign to my fourteen-year-old lounging state as anything could be. I spent the morning squatting at his side, searching for holes and filling them with loose sand and gravel.

Several days after I arrived, my grandfather asked if I wanted to go driving. He would take me to one of the nearby farms. He knew the woman who ran it and she never refused a visitor. He was trying to think up activities. He must have realized that potholes wouldn't keep me going indefinitely and he didn't understand that my favourite way to pass the time was doing nothing. I'd already greased the chains on the hammock.

The farm was owned by a woman called Gwen, who was the county sheriff. When Harry told me this I pictured a stetson and six shooters, but it really meant she sat on committee meetings and made decisions about zoning and the parcelling of property. We turned down the dust road to her farm just as the sun was getting hot. Harry stopped the car near the front porch, got out and stood awkwardly for several seconds. He was very careful about decorum. I think it embarrassed him to call on a woman who was no relation.

He and Gwendolyn had known each other for years. She knew everyone in the area, cottagers included, and made a big point of stopping to say hello and catching up on news when she met people in town or on the road. Harry liked her friendliness. He understood it because of his own farming roots. Petes, who was a city woman, born and bred in Windsor, couldn't stand it. "That woman?" she would say whenever Gwen's name came up. "She's got her finger in everyone's pie."

Gwen appeared on the front doorstep wiping her hands on her jeans. She was a squat woman with silver white hair cropped like an overturned bowl. She looked about as old as Harry but was dressed more like me.

"Harry, you took us by surprise. We were just finishing the breakfast dishes."

I was wondering about the "we" when a thin, childlike person stepped onto the porch. She would have been beautiful except she had a harelip which skewed her face to one side. She didn't say a word, just stared over Gwen's shoulder at us.

Harry got flustered then, said he should have phoned first but he thought they'd be in the garden by now, or working with the bees. Gwen laughed and said they'd slept in. The girl faded back inside the house without saying anything, but Gwen hardly seemed to notice. She came down the stairs for a mid-morning chat.

"Sun for a change," she said looking about her at the yard steeped in light. "The Almanac promises August will be dry." She grinned, taking me in with her violet eyes. Her colours were startling; white hair, eyes dark as huckleberry, skin flushed brown with sun. She knew all about me before I opened my mouth: when I'd arrived, my age, the part of Montreal I came from, the fact I played drums with the band at school.

"Lee plays mandolin. Bluegrass mostly. We've got a

set of bongo drums around here somewhere but neither of us knows how to make them sound good. You should come over some night and jam."

Since when did a woman as old as my grandparents use the word "jam?" She seemed old and young in the same moment. She was wearing jeans and a wine T-shirt. Her breasts hung pendulously underneath. I could see the eraser ends of nipples poking at the cotton. She didn't even have a brassiere on. She looked like someone from my school, yet she was talking credibly with Harry about the state of the roads. He smiled, nodded, thoroughly enchanted. Gwen straddled generations. She was a chameleon, charming whomever happened along.

She spent the morning giving us a tour. At one time she'd owned cows but now the barn was empty except for a sweet-tempered goat called Beulah. She'd sold off most of her pastureland. It was too much work, she said, for the small return. Now all that was left was a vegetable garden and her apiary. The garden was immense, straining at the sides of a mesh wire fence. It could barely be contained. Tomato plants drooped with the weight of pale orange fruit. Someone had placed them beautifully. They were spaced so that each was washed in sunlight.

From far off the garden looked like a quilt. Swatches of colour stopped and started in abrupt lines. Things were arranged as much for the eye as anything else. It was like a collage of origami papers. Gourds and pumpkins grew in one corner. A flame of nasturtiums carpeted the ground beside them. Gossamer fronds of asparagus waved delicately, airy as debutantes. I recognized vegetables when I could find them beneath the leaves and vines, but I was hopeless at naming plants. Gwen raised her eyebrows and said I needed educating.

She told me Lee was mistress of the garden. She'd arrived two years ago from the city knowing as little as I did about the land, but with a book on organic farming strapped to her rucksack. She stopped in the county to look for work. In the two years she'd been with Gwen she'd revolutionized things. They no longer used chemicals; Lee started a compost heap and used only natural pesticides. She planted things Gwen would never have tried: eggplant, herbs, new strains of squash. She also knew how to cook them. Gwen gave Lee free rein in the garden because she was hopeless with bees. She'd tried to train her. That had been the original idea, to get steady help for the apiary, but it hadn't worked out. Every time Lee went near a hive she got stung. At night she dreamt bees were eating her alive. I was secretly glad to hear Lee was fallible. I'd been more than a little awed by Gwen's heaping praise.

By her own account, Gwen was just the opposite of Lee. She'd worked with bees since she was five years old and had never once been stung. It was all in the mind, she said. If a person got scared, the bees sensed it. As long as you were calm and slow they'd let you do anything. She led us through a field in back of the house. At the far end was a row of huts. We stopped several yards away.

"And how are you with bees?" she asked.

One or two flew over to see what we were doing. My underarms turned to water. Sweat rushed down my sides in tepid rivers. I was wearing a pink sweater that day and I'd spritzed on cologne in the bathroom after breakfast. The bees hung suspended in the air around me, considering.

"They seem to like you," Gwen said when neither Harry nor I spoke. "If I were you I'd get rid of the sweater though. They hate getting caught in wool."

I ripped off the sweater and dropped it on the grass. My

arms were bare in a light T-shirt. I felt vaguely like an offering, nubile sacrifice, as we stood in the heat of the noon sun.

The visit was the first of many that summer. Gwen gave me an old bicycle, rusted, without fenders or gears, so I could come and see her on my own. She understood, without a word exchanged between us, that I needed time away from Petes and Harry. My grandparents thought I'd struck up a friendship with Lee, but nothing could be further from the truth. On my first visit alone to the farm, Lee came out onto the porch where Gwen and I were drinking lemonade. She sat on a deck chair and began peeling paint flakes off the armrest.

I watched her hands, which were long and delicately boned. On the left, the nails were clipped short, but on the right she'd let them grow. Dirt was encrusted just below the point where the nail turned white and grew away from the fingertip. Later Gwen told me that Lee liked to keep the nails of one hand long to pluck her mandolin. They looked bad because of all the gardening she did, but they made beautiful sounds.

That day Lee said very little. She listened and seemed to be making up her mind about me. Gwen all but ignored her. Lee's face was narrow, draped on either side by limp black hair. She wore no make-up and her smile, which flashed at rare intervals and faded almost immediately, was marred by surgical scars. It was hard to pin an age on her. At thirteen I was better developed than she was, more fleshy. She was all limbs and bones, skinny as a child. She'd been to university and dropped out, so I guessed she was somewhere in her mid-twenties.

Gwen was talking about bees. She said keeping them was an art; a zen, if you will. At the time I didn't know what zen meant, but I nodded anyways. I kind of got the idea just from her tone. Bees were her passion; caring for them shaped her life. She told a story about collecting honey in a heat wave. It was so hot the sweat dripped in her eyes and slowed the work. Finally, in frustration, she stripped off her shorts and top. A neighbouring farmer, come to visit at dusk, found her at the huts, stark naked except for the boots on her feet.

I laughed at this. I could see her standing in the field, caught out with nowhere to duck and hide. I wasn't used to this kind of talk, to someone sharing past mortifications. In my family, embarrassments were seldom articulated. Adults shrouded themselves in respectable silence.

"She's exaggerating," Lee said. She hadn't said a word until then and I'd forgotten she was there. "She got her T-shirt on before the guy saw anything. She always embellishes."

Gwen was grinning with the recollection. She didn't seem to mind the way Lee tried to shrink the story. I was fuming. I couldn't stand Lee judging everything. She looked like she'd swallowed a quarry of stones and was having problems digesting.

We finished the lemonade and Gwen rose to carry the glasses inside. I followed her and just as she opened the kitchen door, I tripped. I was passing Lee's chair. Her legs were stretched out in front of her, blocking my way and as I stepped over them she jerked them up against one of my shins, hooking my foot and sending me sprawling.

"You okay?" she said neutrally.

I was already on my feet to face her. "Yeah. I guess I'll live."

Gwen hadn't seen. I could hear her running water in the kitchen.

Over the next weeks Gwen initiated me into the world of bees.

I avoided Lee whenever I could. She worked in her garden and I had to be home most days before supper, so our paths didn't cross all that often. About bees I learned many things. I never wore perfume again and I also dressed more simply. Gwen lent me gloves and a net for my head when we visited the hives. She herself only wore gloves. She worked without smoke, most of the time in sleeveless shirts. Her face and arms were exposed and she kept up a constant monologue as bees hovered about her face.

"Bees are so just," she said one day, laughing at the thought. "Everyone has her job. Everyone gets food and shelter. It's probably because they're run by females."

I didn't say much. I was still very nervous and only listened with half an ear. Bees landed on my sleeves, crawled up my pant legs, and it was all I could do to keep from yelling and thrashing out. I prayed fear wouldn't change my smell. Gwen told me how acute the smell sense of a bee was. When Lee came to the hives, for instance, they'd head straight for her, stingers taut and quivering.

One day she spoke unprompted about Lee.

"Her life's been rough. The world is kind only to unblemished packages. You're one of the lucky ones and you can thank the stars for that."

I didn't feel like thanking stars, nor did I forgive Lee. Who cared about her life? I hadn't done her any harm; I stewed with the injustice. It pleased me that the bees scared her off. It meant Gwen and I could have some peace.

Gwen showed me how to lift the tops off hives and how to fix the damaged ones. She explained bee roles in detail.

The queen laid every egg in the hive. All the workers were her daughters. "Imagine the efficiency," Gwen said. "One bee creating an entire world from her womb."

The mating practices dumbfounded me. Ordinarily, Gwen told me, the queen leaves the hive only once for what is called the "nuptial flight." The drones pursue her and four or five eventually catch her. They copulate mid-air, flying beneath her on their backs, and when she's had enough, she kills them. They drop like bombs, lifeless eunuchs spinning through the sky. She is a brutal lover, ripping off the testicles as trophy. Gwen always checked for bee gut hanging from the returning queen.

I loved to listen to Gwen's stories. She made the bees larger than life. A world overflowing with ritual and a violent kind of logic. One day we talked of coronations. One of her hives had lost a queen and she was trying to introduce a new one in larva form.

"It's not certain they'll accept her. They might starve or sting her to death. We'll know in a day or two."

Most often the hive produced its own queen and Gwen didn't have to do it artificially. On rare occasions a new queen was born before the old one died. Then things got hot. Either the old one killed the young one, or else she left. There was never room for two. Gwen said that if I ever saw a swarm travelling in the air, that would be the reason. A sign of *coup d'état*. One queen had forced the other out.

At night on the cot in my grandparents' cottage, I thought about bees. They invaded my dreams. I never was entirely easy with them. At first they terrorized me, crawling on me, smothering me with their whining bodies, but with time I relaxed a little. I was able to appreciate their beauty (their coats were sleek velvet, the gold shimmering like sequins), but my dreams never lost the sharp edge of threat. Once, I had a vision of a gorgeous queen, so huge she had to fold back her wings to fit in my small bedroom. She hung from the ceiling telling me stories. But her gut began to leak, rust-coloured liquid dripped onto my bed. I didn't want to touch it. I knew with the strange intuition of dreams that it was trouble.

It seemed I never spent time with Petes and Harry. The hammock lay abandoned on the lawn, I was too busy with the bees. In contrast to Gwen, my own grandmother seemed faded and pale. It was hard to believe they were the same age. Gwen was self-reliant. She drove a beat-up Ford wagon and delivered honey and vegetables to town herself. The farmers respected her. She could talk with anyone. Petes had to be chauffered by Harry. She only left the house a couple of times a week to replenish her cupboards. She wrote out lists in a girlish script and planned all our suppers in advance. That's how her days were spent so far as I knew, dreaming up menus and worrying that Harry or I would be late to eat.

I didn't know it but I'd half fallen in love with Gwen. I mimicked her smile, the peculiar way she had of rocking on the balls of her feet when she was listening to someone. I began to lisp and swallow the ends of sentences just like she did.

Petes was the first to notice it. We were at dinner, our plates littered with white cobs of corn. Harry and I always competed to see who could eat more. Usually he won with four cobs, but he paid for it. I'd hear him in the bathroom after Petes and I had gone to bed, wrestling with indigestion. That night, he told a long tale about his father's farm. It would have been interesting except he kept bringing in all kinds of bit players, names I'd never heard of. He traced an elaborate tree of family, sisters who married local pastors, brothers long-dead, entire branches of cousins, each with names and dates of birth and death assiduously recorded. He kept notes on family history. One day, he said, he'd pass them onto me. I rolled my eyes. Corpses of flies lay trapped inside the light on the ceiling. Harry didn't see. He never looked at people when he talked. When my eyes rolled down, however, Petes was staring straight at me.

"I suppose I should clear the dishes," I said. Harry's story had stopped.

"You're doing something with your *s's*," Petes chimed. She rarely spoke at meals and even more rarely this directly. "It reminds me of someone." It was so out of character, even Harry was staring at her. "I've got it," she said, excited. "It's Gwen. She's picked up that lisp, exactly like Gwen's."

I could have kicked her. She'd seen it before I noticed it myself.

Three weeks into August, the fields were dry as tinder. The haying had been good, but the farmers were beginning to worry. Everything was yellow, parched. The lake had shrivelled like an old balloon. Rocks lay exposed, their moss skins peeling in the sun. It was marvellous for me. There'd been no rain since the night I arrived from Montreal. I used the bicycle every day and spent most of my time out of doors with the bees.

Summer was ending. The hints were everywhere. The close, damp days of July were long gone and night fell early now, bringing a cold that reached its way under layers of clothing. In less than a week I'd be back in the city. School would start again. A first small wave of nostalgia hit me. What would it be like waking up without the bees?

One morning in my last week at the cottage we were sitting at the breakfast table when the phone rang. It was a party line and Harry always let it ring a few times to make sure it was for us. Two shorts and a long was our code. He picked up the receiver and yelled. Yelling was part of the ritual of the thing; Harry didn't trust that it would work or that a familiar voice would actually make it through the wires. Petes was even worse. She wouldn't touch it. She was convinced the other cottagers listened in on our conversations.

"Who?" Harry shouted. He was squinting as if it might be a crank call. Then his face relaxed. "Oh, Gwen. Didn't sound like you."

I couldn't keep still. I reached for a serviette and sent a glass of juice hurtling across the table. Petes mopped it up, but a plate of toast lay ruined and I'd soaked her table cloth. After interminable minutes Harry hung up, checking the receiver twice to see that the call was over and everything was under control.

"Gwen's off after some runaway bees. She thought you'd like to know."

That was all I needed. I jumped from my chair and began pulling on my tennis shoes. I didn't even stop to lace them. I kissed Petes and Harry and two minutes later I was pedalling furiously along the shoulder of the highway to Gwen's farm.

A queen forced from the nest. It was late in the season for a swarm to be spotted. Frost would soon set in. I pictured Gwen waving a butterfly net. I had no idea how we'd save them.

She was loading things into the back of the Ford when I arrived. I was sweating hard and my hair was tangled from the wind. "You're a sight," she said in her unhurried, lisping way. "Go on into the house and wash up while I finish packing."

It was nine o'clock or so, earlier than I usually arrived and the stillness around Gwen's farm was absolute. The only sounds were the lazy vocals of cicadas in the fields. Lee wasn't in her garden yet. Beulah the goat was nowhere to be seen, probably still sleeping in the barn. I slipped into the kitchen and suddenly a voice came from upstairs.

It was haunting. Unadorned, simple as a boy's. I'd never heard Lee sing. We could barely sit in the same room together, let alone think of making music. I thought of her as thoroughly hateful, an ugly creature. Yet here was this voice, the sweetness trapped inside her. I didn't turn on the faucet. I just stood and listened, and that's how Gwen found me when she came in from outside. "Oh," she said, her face going all soft as if someone had struck her. "She's really something, isn't she."

We drove west to the far edge of the county. A man out there had seen the swarm and phoned Gwen because he knew she kept bees. The law said that anyone who captured a swarm on the wing could claim title, Gwen explained as we sped past fields of splintered cornstalks.

They were just where he said they'd be, on a tree in the back of a dilapidated farmhouse. The tree was small and from far off the bees looked like a cluster of grapes dangling from an upper branch. The reality of our task hit me then. Gwen and I would have to capture this crawling, whining mass of life, move it into the Ford and drive with it for at least a half hour over rough dirt roads. I don't know what I'd been imagining. I guess I never expected we'd find them.

Gwen took a large sheet out of the car and spread it under the tree. She could have been preparing a picnic except for the angry buzzing at her head. The bees tolerated her, sending low warnings as she worked. She took pruning shears and deftly, in a single motion, snapped the branch about a foot above the swarm. It dropped heavily onto the centre of the sheet.

The bees spun in crazy orbit. Like planets with displaced magnetic fields. Gwen and I were statues. Neither of us moved; our breath slowed to the minimum. We didn't dare look at each other until finally the bees began to quiet and regroup about the queen on the severed branch.

Gwen passed me the shears. Then delicately, as if she were tucking in a sleeping child, she lifted a corner of the bedsheet and laid it over her prize. We did this with each corner, tiptoeing around the perimeter of the sheet, until the bees were folded safely away. There was still a hissing noise but it was muffled and the white surface gave the illusion that the bees had vanished.

On the drive back to the farm, Gwen turned to me. Bees hummed from the back seat. Six or seven had crawled out and hung suspended in the air inside the car. They crashed their small bodies against the windshield, unable to make sense of this transparent wall.

"You were marvellous," Gwen said. "Nothing fazes you." I grinned with a lopsided grin that wasn't quite my own, lapping up the praise. "I wish I could keep you here. Between us we'd get that apiary cooking."

I'd never been so happy. Visions of me living in the big old house somersaulted in my mind. I dropped Lee from the picture. She was the one dark spot, of course. Maybe Gwen would invite me back to work next summer and by that time Lee would have moved on. We drove slowly. Gwen turned on the radio and the rasping voice of Bob Dylan filled the car. I'd first heard of Dylan only two years before. I remember some kid playing *Lay Lady Lay* in class in sixth grade. There was plenty of static. Gwen said the bees wouldn't mind. It was probably opera to them.

When we pulled into the yard, Lee came running from

the garden. She was smiling but she stopped several yards off when she saw I was there. Gwen yelled to stay away and told briefly about the swarm. She patted my arm and said I'd been a star. Lee turned without saying anything, without any congratulations or any soft word, and walked off, sullen, inscrutable, back to her work.

I didn't see Gwen for three days after that. It had rained steadily and I'd been helping Harry close up the cottage. I couldn't take the bicycle out and the walk was too long. I'd phoned once to let her know I was alive, but she and Lee must have been out. There was no answer.

The evening before I left for Montreal, I pedalled over to her place. The house was dark and empty-looking but the Ford was there, a sign that she was in. I ran up the steps, calling her name. The door to the kitchen was unlatched. No one locked their doors here. Gwen said it was rude. What if visitors came by and you weren't in? At least then they could leave a note on your table or fix themselves a juice. Through the screen I saw dishes and some papers on the counter, as if someone had eaten and not bothered to clean up. I called again.

It was past eight and the sky was turning a watery brown. Maybe she was off in the fields with Lee or perhaps she'd gone to check her bees. I decided she couldn't be far and that the best idea was to wait on the porch. I sat on one of the peeling chairs, tugging the sleeves of my sweater down over my hands. The night was clear and a crescent moon, amber-coloured and spongey like comb honey, hung low in the sky.

The air had that fresh quality that comes after rain. I could smell gum on the trees and the green of the fields was deep, saturated now that water had touched the land. The soil would be teeming with insect life. I sat hugging my knees, feeling cold crawl up the surface of my skin. And then I heard Gwen. There were no words, just sounds, low, repetitive, breaking the still night.

I was rooted to the chair. It was a slow dawning. Gwen and Lee. A truth I'd known somehow, but never dared to look at. I closed my eyes but the sounds kept on, insistent, pushing through.

After a while I got up to go. I must have made noise because someone raised a window directly above me and light streamed onto the porch.

"Who's there?" Lee's voice, timid in the night.

I sidestepped the shaft of light and ran. I didn't speak. Didn't care if I was seen. The bicycle was leaning against Gwen's car exactly where I'd left it, but I ran on, straight to the highway. The only sound was my feet on gravel; even the crickets had stopped their song. And all the way home that August night the moon's grin followed me, glinting above the tree branches, ageless, vaguely mocking.

Beyond The Pale

In the middle of my last year of primary school, the moving vans came. I'll never forget it. It was winter, early February, and that last morning we were sent off to school with written instructions so we could return to the new house. I was to wait for my younger brother, Marty, to make sure he didn't get lost.

For weeks, my mother had been preparing. The walls of our house were already stripped bare, the mirrors and paintings wrapped in layers of tissue and plastic. The walls were scarred with squares, ovals, holes from nails my father hammered in years ago. It looked lonely, bereft, days before we left. I loved this house. We'd lived here eleven years, the entire span of my life, and leaving it felt like betrayal. It wasn't particularly big or beautiful. A modest semi-detached in red brick with a patch of grass behind. But it had its charms. A garden that while small, was also private, ringed with walls of lilac; an attic for playing. It was very near my school and the back door was always swinging and slamming with children.

Our neighbours were an elderly man, Mr Angus, and his wife. Their side of the house was painted white. It looked strange, the white and red together stood out on our quiet, middleclass street. An aesthetic statement (about what I'm not quite sure), something to jolt the eye.

Mrs Angus was an invalid. I remember being told not to make noise or I'd disturb her. One early memory is of me squatting in a flower bed in our garden. I must have been three or four. It was summer and I was chewing dirt. I knew it was wrong, I'd been told a hundred times, but there was so much of it, sun-warmed, deeply black, and it tempted me badly. The dirt exploded against my teeth. It was like cannons inside my head, blasts of trumpets announcing the misdemeanor. Something dark moved above me and I looked up with the instinct of a small ground creature. It was Mr Angus on his roof terrace. I froze, mortified, convinced my chewing had awoken him.

The wood panels next to my bed were patterned with scallops. They dated back to when I was one. Mr Angus had a train set in the room directly adjacent to mine. My mother deduced this because certain afternoons it sounded as if the Canadian Pacific was about to burst through the wall. Whistles screamed, engines strained, wheels clattered along iron tracks. At one year old I didn't yet discern between the imaginary and real, and my small heart used to gallop. I defended myself as best I could, lying back on the bed, raising booted feet to the wall and kicking for all I was worth. Those scallops were my infant terror.

I was leaving this behind. Little chunks of my life embedded in the rooms. I'd seen the new house only once. It was enormous, entirely detached, and surrounded by extensive grounds on the top of a steep hill. Montreal has two hills situated in the centre of the island. The biggest one, Mount Royal, is a dead volcano. This impressed me when I was small; I was afraid one day it would come to life. Our new house was on the smaller incline, Westmount Mountain, where many of the city's wealthy English families lived.

My bedroom had a balcony that looked south across the city, and for the first time I had the sense of living on an island. I could see the river with miniature ships inching down towards the ocean. The greys and browns of Montreal ended abruptly at the water's edge. I knew it was dirty, raw sewage was constantly flooding the river basin, but it looked beautiful. Soft blues and greens glinting in the sun. On good days I made out the contours of the Adirondacks across the border. I could see for miles.

From the balcony, I watched storms. With the first cracks of thunder I'd slip outside and watch them spread across the city. The best ones were like sheets of something solid, glass maybe or metal, and they swept the sky with violent brush strokes. I loved to watch them rush towards me, chasing the dry air out in front, engulfing the city street by street until finally they arrived to swallow me, the garden, the house, in a torrent of driving water.

As spectacular as the view was, I hated our new home. It swamped us. We didn't have furniture to fill it. The half-empty rooms made me feel like a stranger, a newcomer years after we'd moved in. What's more, there were no children on our street. That far up the mountain the houses were huge and costly. It was a place people retired to.

The winter of the move was hard for me in a number of ways. There was dislocation, leaving the house of my birth and childhood, but there were also things going on inside me that filled me with confusion. It was the winter I grew five inches and blossomed, while I still felt so much a child, into an alarming, early womanhood. All of a sudden my body took on the airs of a seventeen-year old. Public workers and men in cars began ogling me when I stepped outside. I towered above my schoolmates who were still skinny and sexless and walked undisturbed on their ways home from school. I also seemed to have lost control of my limbs. I couldn't reach out an arm without some object tumbling and breaking. My knees buckled on stairs and my mother would rush out from the kitchen to find me in a stunned, slightly bruised heap, grinning stupidly on the landing.

My mother didn't often comment about these changes. In one sense I was glad no one called attention to my metamorphosing self, but I was also very lonely. I had no idea that it was just one of life's stages, that it would pass, that eventually I'd get back my balance, a steadier sense of self. School was brutal. I was already in a brassiere, furtively stuffing kotex into pencil cases while my girlfriends were flat-chested and free as boys. In the locker room before gym they giggled as I changed shirts. Cruel jokes were made about menstruation. I tried not to listen and kept myself well-hidden.

My brother, Marty, slept on the opposite side of the house from me, overlooking the road. One morning in February, just after we'd moved in, he did something that went down in the family annals. Boxes were still piled high in the hallways. Stray furniture sat awkwardly waiting to be placed. The front doorbell wasn't working. The wires had been cut and my father hadn't got around to fixing them. It was Sunday and my parents were still sleeping. Marty was playing in his room when he heard the voice. At first he couldn't tell where it was coming from. It was a man's voice, familiar although very faint, calling his name. He went to the window and there below him, standing in the snow, was Zeyda.

Zeyda was my father's dad. He was a small man without a hair on his head. Marty stared down at the gleaming surface of scalp, now mottled with cold. Zeyda was, by nature, hairy.

Grey tufts curled out the neck of his shirts and covered his arms and hands. When the hair on his head started to thin he grew worried. He'd never liked half measures, so he asked the barber to shave it off. "Why not go all the way?" he'd said when we first saw it. Someone had told him it turned women on.

My father was embarrassed by Zeyda. It wasn't just the way he looked, the bald head which he flaunted even in winter, it was the way he talked, the things he did. My mother said he didn't know better. He came from Poland at sixteen, speaking Yiddish and one or two words of English. He didn't know Polish. That was for gentiles and educated people. His accent was thick, full of tongue and lips. In Poland, he'd lived by scavenging. He was from a large, fatherless family and he'd hawked things in the street, bartering odds and ends he'd found for turnips, potatoes, anything to feed the mouths at home. His story read like a dimestore novel. He landed in Montreal penniless, barely literate, a boy with a cumbersome, foreign name and a Communist Party card in one pocket. Within three years, he'd burned the card and dropped several syllables from the name. By the end of his first decade, a fleet of women worked for him, cutting, stitching in a north-end sweatshop. He declared a holy war on unions, and shortly thereafter, announced to the world that he'd made his first million.

That was Zeyda. Rags to riches in the flesh.

Zeyda was waving a brown bag, talking and gesticulating. Marty couldn't make out the words. His window was closed, but still, he knew exactly what Zeyda wanted and even what was in the bag. He didn't budge. He shook his head slowly at the old man and watched him climb back into his car and drive away.

Zeyda had brought bagels from Saint Viateur Street and wanted to be let in. He'd knocked and pushed the bell, he told them later, but no one had heard. Then he'd started calling up to Marty's room. It was a Sunday ritual. Zeyda used to drop by the old house with hot bagels and cream cheese and they'd invite him in for an hour or so. He figured he'd surprise them this first Sunday at the new place, but it didn't work out.

My father was furious when he learned what had happened. He scolded Marty and asked what on earth had come over him. Marty went shy and wordless, as he often did when he'd been bad, and wouldn't say what was going through his head. But I knew. I knew the moment I heard the story. Marty was just aping Father. Pushing Zeyda away.

Zeyda was a widower. My grandmother, Rose, died the year I was born and I only knew her through anecdote. Zeyda still occupied the family house. It was huge, even bigger than our new one and not far away. He had to hire a truck to plow the driveway that curved endlessly up from the street. There were five bedrooms upstairs, only one of them lived in. The others were furnished for ghosts. Sheets draped the furniture, heavy curtains stopped the light. My father's old bedroom was apparently intact under layers of white shroud, exactly as it had been when he was young. A black lady called Carmen lived in the attic. She cooked and kept the place in order. She spoke with an Islands accent and her dark eyes were always lowered, meekly darting.

Marty and I didn't mind visits to Zeyda's. There was a colour television (in those days, still a rarity) and a weight loss machine upstairs. You attached the belt around your hips, leaned back, and it jiggled you, supposedly to a smaller, more desirable shape. There was also a bench, and a set of barbells.

We amused ourselves for hours while the grown ups talked below.

Miniature plum trees grew on the front lawn. The fruit were small and purple, and dozens of them lay rotting on the ground because Zeyda couldn't eat them all. Marty and I waged war with Zeyda's plums every autumn. We positioned ourselves behind hedges, behind cars parked on the hill and hurled the soft fruit at each other. Already Marty's pitch was better than mine. I threw awkwardly, without aim, whereas my brother, as if by the magic of his gender, swung in a perfect line. He seldom missed his target.

Zeyda filled boxes with plums and tried to convince us to take them home. He hated to see waste; his Polish past had seared him with a lifelong frugality. "It's free," he'd say. "You could make pies." And when Marty and I shook our heads and continued to play, he'd shrug as if he didn't understand. The plums were good for wars but I couldn't bring myself to eat them. The flesh was dry and somewhat mealy. They weren't at all like the imported ones my mother bought at the grocer's. What's more, they looked vulgar, like the turds of a dog littering the fresh-cut grass.

At Zeyda's, dinners were elaborate. The table was always beautifully set with silver and fine linen. There were cloth napkins in pewter rings and a confusing array of spoons and forks and knives. It was at Zeyda's that I learned to use the small fork for my salad, the rounded one for fish, the small knife for my cheese and fruit. We dined well there. Carmen would come into the dining room with steaming plates of roast. Then she would pour wine like my dead grandmother had taught her, with the napkin draped over one arm. Zeyda directed her, yelling orders to the kitchen. He even had a bell, hidden under the rug at his end of the table, which he could ring when he wanted her.

When the food arrived, he picked up a spoon or fork from the vast array of implements around his plate and fed himself quickly and clumsily. Somehow, despite the candelabra, the china and silver, Zeyda remained awkward. Some things mark a man forever, and one of them I got the feeling, was poverty. Zeyda could never learn to savour food, to draw out a meal with talk as my parents liked to do. For him, food was food and mealtimes were for eating. He'd grown accustomed to a well-set table, but it was all the same so long as he filled his belly.

My family scorned him. It was the way he ate, but it was also that he'd say anything at the table. One evening, not long after the episode with Marty and the bagels, we were dining together. It was the Sabbath and my mother had just finished reciting the blessing over the candles. The amen was barely out of her mouth when Zeyda began talking about how grown up I was getting. I'd just started wearing a brassiere that month and I knew he was referring to it. Earlier, he'd rubbed my back lightly with the palm of his hand as if he'd seen, and was proud.

"She's no longer a child," he said, nodding meaningfully at my father. "Soon you'll be fending off the men."

I went scarlet. My cheeks burned like the candles my mother had just lit. Marty began to snigger. Most of the time I tried to ignore my body, or at the very least minimize its existence. My father and mother connived with me on this. They didn't want to face my transmutations any more than I did. A pall of silence hung over my clumsiness, the way I hurtled down staircases. Talk of undergarments or the fact that I'd started my periods was absolutely taboo. Whether or not

Zeyda understood this unspoken pact, I can't say, but it was clear he wasn't about to join it. At the time I could do nothing but hate him. Strings of the worst epithets I knew thrashed in my mind. It would be years before I could appreciate his gesture that night; I had so much more to learn about bodies.

Eventually the furniture got sorted in the new house. My father hammered hooks into the walls and hung our paintings. We had to buy more furniture to fill the rooms, but for a long time it seemed unfinished, as if something were missing. I got used to it in time. I passed the old house only occasionally. Unfamiliar curtains hung in the windows, a strange car stood sentry in the driveway. A couple of times I saw blonde children, much younger than me, playing on the strip of grass in front.

When I was fourteen I finally stopped growing. It happened suddenly, as if a good witch tapped me with her wand. My limbs became my own again. I joined a gymnastics club, revelling in my new-found grace. It wasn't the rough, quick grace of childhood; that was gone forever. But precision had returned; once more I knew the arc and reaches of my body. I did stairs without a slip. Things had also improved at school. My classmates had caught up to me. By that time most of them had grappled with that hard sliver of age where girl bodies change to women. Brassieres were prestige items. Busts were now in vogue. I was long past the agonizing changeling stage. I still looked older than I was, but I could handle it a little better. Zeyda proved right about fending off men. My father had to set curfews on how late telephone calls could come through. It seemed I was in demand.

  In April, just as a hesitant spring was breaking in

Montreal, Zeyda came up from Florida. He spent winters there, leaving in the autumn after the Jewish New Year, and arriving back in spring to celebrate Passover. He had a condominium (a word I'd learned recently and couldn't utter without blushing) just off the ocean. I'd never been down, but he told us it was lovely. Pelicans, with beaks like great shovels, flew overhead. The sunsets were like exploding furnaces, hot red and purple drenching the sky. He had a garden with trees that gave fruit the entire time he was there: grapefruits the size of footballs and as sweet as if you'd poured on sugar, oranges, avocados.

I was studying in my room when he dropped over, unannounced. From the distance he looked yellow. He stood in the middle of our living-room wearing a turquoise pullover, his skin luminescent with contrasting colour. My father and mother looked white as porcelain beside him.

Recently I'd begun to think about his life. He'd never spoken about his youth and I'd never thought to ask, but I'd been reading a little about Russia and Poland in school. The Pale, that was where Zeyda was from. Ghetto for the Jews. Now, he began to intrigue me. He'd crossed galaxies to reach the house on the summit of Westmount. After all, he'd come when he was still a boy, not knowing a soul, not knowing the language. He had no idea of customs, of the people, the climate he'd find. He was sixteen, a year and a half older than I was then.

He walked over to me and gave me a noisy kiss. Up close he looked frailer than I remembered. The tan only partially hid age, a host of minor infirmities. I was taller by a few inches and I could see the light dancing off his scalp. He was holding something and he passed it to me. An opaque bag, tightly knotted, which had obviously made the journey with him from

Florida. Marty moved in then, to see if there would be further presents. He was at that age where things interested him much more than people. But Zeyda had nothing else. He just tousled Marty's hair and said it was too long for a boy, he should go and see a barber. Marty made a sour face and scrutinized the bag.

When I finally got the knot untied, Zeyda said, "They're from my garden." I pulled out two enormous avocados. My mother cooed that they were lovely, and told Zeyda what a green thumb she thought he had, but I just stood there for a second as if I'd never seen an avocado before. The skins were dark and blistered. They were obscenely large.

"I had to smuggle them in," he said, as if this would increase their value. I was disappointed. I didn't like the way he skimped on gifts, no matter what kind of a past he'd had. At least he could have brought American chocolate or even the cheap make-up kits he'd given me as a child.

My father offered drinks and Zeyda said he'd have Dubonnet. He wasn't supposed to. It was bad for his sugar, he told us. But it was the holiday season, after all, you could only expect so much from a man. I said I wanted some too. "No way," Marty piped out immediately. His back was turned and he was playing with a set of antique pistols that hung on the wall for decoration. "If she gets some, so do I." Father gave me a weary look as if I should have foreseen this, but in the end, relented and went to fix shot glasses heavily diluted with water.

Zeyda asked me and Marty about school and we answered perfunctorily. These meetings were always strained, a duty to be got through. He talked to fill the silence, asking about the winter, telling us how he missed snow. All his life he'd lived in the northern hemisphere. He couldn't get used to Florida which wiped out entire seasons. Years went by faster, he claimed, when there was no change to punctuate them. He went south for his health, but the only thing that got him through the winter was the garden. It was a miracle to grow things all year round. "Look outside," he said. "The buds aren't even open here, but yesterday I plucked avocados from my tree."

The Dubonnet and talk soon took their toll and Zeyda excused himself and went to the toilet. He had to climb stairs to get to it. It was surprising but our house, large and impressive as it was, had only one bathroom. Guests had to climb up to the second floor to freshen up. We shared it with my parents. There was no latch on the door and one or the other of us was constantly barging in. It was all right to do it to my mother, everyone did. She would smile and begin conversations. Father, however, was a different story. How often had I come upon him in the morning, hunched over on the toilet in a cloud of incriminating smells. I would back off as if the doorknob had turned to molten lead. Whenever I used the bathroom I always kept one foot braced against intruders.

Zeyda didn't reappear for some time. My mother told my father in a low whisper how old he was looking. He'd grown thinner. It wasn't a good sign at his age. My father listened silently. He was never easy when Zeyda was around.

At last Zeyda came back down the stairs, taking them one at a time as old men do, and walked into the middle of the room. He turned slowly, like a model on display. "It happens sometimes when you're old," he said, shrugging.

I didn't know what he was going on about. We stared at him, not understanding. And then I saw it. A dark stain creeping down his pantleg, blackening it from crotch to knee. My mother began to laugh in loud, embarrassed peals. Marty and even Father joined her. Zeyda had peed his pants. I laughed too, I couldn't keep it down, and soon we were all sitting there, shaking helplessly, watching the old man through teary eyes.

Zeyda kept his smile. After the laughter died down he sat and talked for several more minutes. My eyes kept travelling to the leg, and I imagined the way the skin would feel under the damp wool. Clammy, slightly prickly with the acid. No one offered a towel or a change of clothes. We were like school kids, aware of guilt but not knowing how to right it. Zeyda talked about his sugar. He explained that sometimes he lost control. Bodies were like that, he said. It was just part of life.

I felt really bad then. As though Zeyda was the most dignified person I knew. I thought of saying it was okay, a bit of urine wasn't the end of the world, but before I could get it out of my mouth, it was too late. He was on his feet, heading for the vestibule. Father followed, helped him on with his jacket. After the door closed we looked at each other but no one could think of anything to say.

A few days later, Zeyda came to our house for Seder dinner. My mother had laid a lavish table. We too had a heavy candelabrum which she lit, raising her hands in prayer. There were dishes of herbs, apples mixed with nuts and wine, bowls of salt water to symbolize Jewish tears. My mother prepared the same meal every year. It was a ritual with her, as unvarying as the seasons. This year she made a slight alteration. As an entrée we were served spears of avocado dipped in lemon vinaigrette. They looked wonderful on the plate, curved moons gleaming against the china. The flesh melted like butter when I put it in my mouth.

Zeyda was in good spirits. I remember him telling me to

keep the pits. If I wanted, I could start a Quebec strain of his fruit. I did salvage them. I'm not sure why I did this. I'd never grown anything before and plants didn't interest me, but I cleaned and dried them and kept them in my socks drawer for months. To tell you the truth, I'd forgotten all about them when the phone call came through from Florida telling us Zeyda had suffered a stroke.

Zeyda never really got strong again. It was one complication after another. We moved him back to Montreal and my parents cared for him as best they could, but he'd lost all movement on one side of his body, and his speech was as laboured as a child's. He kept slipping into Yiddish and expecting us to understand.

Some time after his death I remembered the avocados. It was my last year at home before I left for college and I recall taking them from the drawer and soaking them. They expanded with the water, their skins sloughing off, and then a white root burst through to split each stone. I planted them and they sat out on my balcony all that summer, drinking in sun and city fumes, and thriving. When I moved away I carted them with me, first to anonymous campus residences, and later to a series of student flats. Someone told me that in Canada the sun was too weak and I could never hope for avocados; but I did hope. I gave them food and water and plenty of light, and they grew tall and sturdy. And even though, in the end, they didn't bear fruit, I was never disappointed. They fill my rooms with an arching, junglish kind of beauty which pleases me to this day.

Salad Days

The town where she had her first love affair was not the most likely or romantic spot. It was nothing more spectacular than a cluster of farms and houses strung out along a highway, but Rachel was sixteen, and at that age it was easy to make even Saint Aurélie a place of beauty and intrigue.

Saint Aurélie was a farming town, not particularly orderly or carefully kept. Smells from the pigs and chickens attracted thick clouds of flies each summer. Every house in the area was infested with them, not to mention the church, and the roadside diner with the words *poutine* and *chien chaud* scrawled in a child's hand on its sign. At the western end of town, a strip of asphalt split off from the highway, climbed a hill and frayed like an old piece of rope into a system of unpaved, country roads.

When Rachel first arrived, the smallness disconcerted her. Everyone had porches, and in the evening they brought chairs out so they could watch the sun going down, and keep an eye on children who played a whisper away from the highway. They also watched the other balconies and talked among themselves, starting new rumours or rehashing old, familiar ones. Rachel wasn't used to the slow pace, or to everyone's poking into everyone else's business. Talk would stop as she walked by; eyes would follow her. She never caught them looking, but she could feel it.

She was in Saint Aurélie that summer on a program to learn French. There were twelve of them staying in the town, living with families who had agreed to take them in. Rachel was the youngest of the group. She was also the only person from Quebec. The others were from places like Medicine Hat, Alberta or the Kootenays. Some were teachers, some were still in university. One man, Grant Niles, a young high school teacher from British Columbia, chastised her for not being fluent. He loved French and spoke it every chance he got. Out West, he said, the chances were dismally few. He envied Rachel, who could walk into any store or restaurant in Montreal and speak a foreign language.

Rachel had never regarded things in this light before. She didn't mind French, but it was like any subject served up at school, just one more way to fill an afternoon. Her teachers spoke with shrill, clipped accents, straight from Paris or some colony in North Africa, and she was taught an idiom that was foreign and stilted in the context of her home. Before that summer, Rachel never found any use for French. It was difficult to explain. She lived in a French city, in the middle of an almost purely French province, but until her sixteenth year it was just something she had to study, with as little value as trigonometry or the periodic table.

She lived in an English neighbourhood and at the time, Montreal was divided into ghettos. The barriers were so deep that it was possible for a girl like her to grow through an entire childhood and never utter a French word.

Learning French wasn't all that painful in the end. She had a head full of dormant grammar: structures drilled into her and stored away over the years. She got over her shyness with the new sounds and was soon stringing words like so many beads. She was staying with the grocer and his family, and not one of them spoke English. Their name was Grondin. There were four girls, the eldest of whom, Gina, was just a bit younger than Rachel. They all helped with the store, and in the hottest month of summer, harvested strawberries on a farm just down the highway. Gina was dark like Madame Grondin. Marie, the second daughter was physical and full of bad jokes like her father. The youngest two were hard to tell apart. They were both very skinny, with olive skin and round, protruding eyes.

When Madame Grondin first heard about the course, she wanted nothing to do with it. She was very protective and didn't want her daughters corrupted by city people. Besides, several years before, she and her husband drove the entire family through Ontario in a rented trailer. It was a disaster. She told Rachel she couldn't ask the simplest things, where the toilet was, for example, or how much for a coke, without trouble and misunderstandings. No one west of the border helped them, or addressed them in their own language. Ottawa was all right, she said, but even there, in the capital, there were many people who didn't understand her. If she accepted a boarder she was convinced that either Gina would get seduced, or a full-scale language war would erupt. Finally, after weeks of leaning over her counter, talking with the other women in town, she decided it wouldn't be so bad after all. She insisted though, for the sake of her girls, and especially for Gina, who was being groomed for studies in the big town fifty kilometres west of her home, that her boarder be female, and the very youngest person in the group.

Rachel couldn't have been luckier. The family was good and gentle, and the parents were accustomed to girls. Food was always fresh because it was the Grondins' business. They ate beef from the vault freezer in the store, and mushrooms that Madame Grondin fried in a pan with garlic and sizzling butter. The store was the hub of village life. Most rumours started there, with Madame Grondin disappearing behind the bread rack to whisper with her women friends, sending the little girls out into the sunshine, out of earshot, while the news was culled and sorted.

Rachel slept in a room with a double bed. Her window looked out over a large tract of land that didn't belong to the Grondins. An old man worked it early in the morning with a starved-looking horse. The room was decorated with ornaments of the kind found in tea boxes and game booths at fairs. A cancan girl kicked up her heels on one corner of the dresser. Beside her, a collection of birds sat in a docile row. Tiny, gold-painted hens pecked the dresser's surface. Larger ones, with translucent porcelain feathers, sat complacently nearby. They were hollow creatures with small bowls hidden inside and their backs lifted easily, like pot covers. They weren't just ornamental, one of the younger girls explained to Rachel; they could be used as dishes for eggs at breakfast. Someone had gone to considerable trouble collecting, placing them, and keeping them free from dust.

The thing in the room that impressed Rachel most was the crucifix hanging at the foot of her bed. Its face was bluish white, as if it were dead or desperately ill. The head lolled forward under cruel thorns and lines of blood seeped down its cheeks, and its abdomen and thigh. Rachel had never seen a crucifix close up. Her family didn't make much of religion and she'd been inside a church only once, when her youngest aunt got married.

The little girls came to her room each night before bed. They were extremely shy, and at first Rachel didn't understand. She thought they just wanted to visit. But then the youngest slid to her knees in front of the icon and began to say prayers. The room belonged to the two youngest Grondins. It was they who collected the hens and cheap dolls, and they who tended the bruised and bleeding Christ. They trotted in each night to recite their prayers, and knelt down unabashedly, shutting their eyes in front of the wall.

On her first Sunday in Saint Aurélie, the Grondins brought her to Mass. Everyone in the family washed that morning. Gina wore stockings, and black heeled shoes, ignoring the heat. Even Marie changed from her usual garb of overalls. They sat together in a pew several rows from the front. Madame Grondin was at the aisle. Her girls assembled themselves in a line of decreasing age. First Gina, then Marie, then the young ones, and finally, at the far end of the pew, Monsieur Grondin, to control any giggling or fights. Gina sat quietly through the service, her dark eyes following the *curé* as he moved about the altar. Two seats down, Marie could not keep still. She was craning her neck and making faces at a boy in the pew behind them.

The sermon was about love. The *curé* was a small man who took great pleasure in waving his hands. They fluttered like pigeons in the soft morning light. Rachel stared up at rose and purple glass and tried to remember Bible stories. She couldn't imagine how the little Grondins kept from fidgeting. Every once in a while Monsieur Grondin popped peppermints into their mouths, but Rachel knew that candy alone was not enough.

The *curé* spoke for almost an hour. "Love," he said, "isn't only a thing of the flesh." Marie started to snigger and received a daggered look from Madame Grondin. Everyone, he said, made so much of the love between man and woman, but this was only the smallest bit of what it was. Rachel studied the backs of heads. Rows of them, the hair combed, slicked back, some bald, the necks burnt black by sun. She let the words fall about her, scattering, weightless in the great hall.

Every Sunday after that first one, the Grondins performed the ritual of walking down the dusty highway to church. Rachel was always two steps ahead, with excuses to get out of it.

The river was only a few miles from town. Saint Aurélie was quite far east near the gulf, and the water was so wide it was like the ocean, washing against the shore in regular tides. The sand was draped with seaweed and purslane that tasted strongly of salt. On Sundays and some weekdays after class, she walked down to the beaches. She loved it by the water. She'd never been near an ocean before, and the immensity and greyness made her wistful, her heart going suddenly soft like some pulsing sea plant.

It was on the beaches that she thought about Grant Niles. She didn't dare show it in class and she wouldn't have admitted it to anyone, but she'd fallen in love. She turned red-faced, inarticulate when he walked into the room, and when he wasn't around, her mind was constantly conjuring him. She never dreamt for a moment that he would love her back. He was twenty-three, for one thing. Everyone in the class looked up to him. He was from the west and was affable and outgoing. She, on the other hand, was just out of an eastern city high school, young, tongue-tied half of the time.

Every morning they read *Poussiere sur la Ville*. There weren't enough copies to go around, and she and Grant had to share. The novel was all about southern Quebec and the cancer that kills off miners and their families working in asbestos towns there. Grant mentioned that one summer he'd worked in a mine. She was so awed by this fact, this scrap of story from his past, that she forgot to ask him what it was like, or why he did it, or what kind of mine it had been. She just stared at him and smiled stupidly and blushed. She had no idea what he thought of her.

One afternoon, on the pretext of needing *Poussiere sur la Ville,* she borrowed Marie's bicycle and went into the back roads behind the town. This was where Grant lived. He was staying on a farm where they fed him almost nothing but mashed potatoes and white bread. The people weren't friendly, he said, and he was getting hives from the starch. The farms up in this area were far from the road and every house had a dog which came tearing down its long driveway, barking like mad as she passed. She had to build up speed and pedal really hard to escape.

Grant's place was guarded by a doberman. A fleshy lady came out of the house when she arrived because of all the racket it was making. She didn't apologize for the animal or even ask what Rachel wanted. Grant stepped into the yard a minute later, saw the dog, then Rachel, and rushed over to see if she were all right. Ordinarily, his face didn't show much emotion. In class she couldn't tell if he was mocking or friendly, but that afternoon was different. He told her not to mind the dog, and whispered that the same went for the woman, and she laughed shyly. The woman watched them, not saying a word as they walked into the fields behind the house. Rachel began to recover. She chattered about farm dogs and the thrill of cycling the rough back roads. They spoke in French and their language was broken, fragmented; at least Rachel felt hers was, but this made the walk somehow more extraordinary. They crossed stubbled grass, climbing through barbed wire set up between the lots of land, and for the first time, Grant seemed really pleased with her.

Two days later in the Grondins' store, Rachel recognized the lady from Grant's farm. Three loaves of the bland bread he complained of were piled in her shopping cart, and she was reaching for more. The bread was stacked on top of an immense sack of animal meal. Rachel cursed her. How could she expect a man like Grant to survive on that? She got a stipend from the government for board, but by the looks of it she spent it all on her dog.

Madame Grondin went to help her and soon the two of them were whispering furiously. The woman had not caught sight of Rachel, playing checkers with Marie near the cash.

"Looks like hot new gossip," Marie observed, motioning with her chin to her mother. Marie was only twelve, but she had a coolness about her much like Monsieur Grondin's; she pretended she was above female chatter and concerns. Madame Grondin's head appeared over the top of the rack and she glared at Rachel. The discussion started up again with even more frenzy.

In the kitchen that evening, Rachel helped Madame Grondin and Gina fix a salad. They worked in silence. The only noise was the low buzz from the television set which the Grondins left on in their living-room from dawn until they went to their rooms to sleep. Sometimes they would leave it on all night and Rachel would waken to sounds of canned laughter or music echoing through the hallway.

"The other day when you took Marie's bicycle, you didn't say you were going visiting," Madame Grondin said.

Rachel didn't answer. The look on Gina's face said this was serious, that her mother was upset.

"You were up at the Vachons," Madame Grondin persisted. Gina, who knew the family, and couldn't understand what on earth Rachel would want at the Vachon farm, stared at her.

"You *were* there, weren't you?" Madame Grondin crushed the ends of two carrots against the rough, serrated metal, just missing her thumb. "Madame Vachon came this afternoon. She told me." The grater slipped from Madame Grondin's hands. "She doesn't want girls coming to visit her boarders."

Rachel's cheeks grew hot. She was shy with Madame Grondin, but she was also proud. The two women had actually discussed where she went. They seemed to care whom she visited.

"You're a good girl," Madame Grondin said kindly, mistaking the silence for shame. "But around here you must be careful. People talk."

Rachel's chin quivered. She'd never heard of such a thing. At home she could come and go as she pleased. All of a sudden, she hated Saint Aurélie, hated the smallness, the women who gathered in the Grondin store to swap stories. She hated Gina who sat in church pews learning ways that would strangle her before she dared put a foot outside her door. That was how Rachel saw it then, amid the carrot peels and odours of roasting meat in Madame Grondin's kitchen.

They ate supper as usual, but Rachel had lost trust in the Grondin women. In her mind she allied herself with Grant, who withstood his lot up at the Vachon farm, and continued to charm her and make her laugh in class. He had no time for gossip or spending his Sundays in church.

One Saturday, the Grondins took her to a dance in a town not far away. The whole family went, even the little girls, dressed in skirts and white knee socks. The dance was in honour of the 150th anniversary of the town, and there was plenty of wine and a live band with an accordion. It was a damp night, cool and drizzling, and everyone crowded under a large striped canvas tent. Rachel was sipping wine and listening to Monsieur Grondin's jokes when Gina took her arm and pulled her into the crowd. The dance floor was packed and they had to walk almost the width of the tent to find space. The band started playing a slow, waltzy tune and Gina turned to Rachel and drew her close, holding her as if she were a man. Rachel was deeply embarrassed. She laughed and tried to draw back, but Gina persisted. It was only then that she noticed they weren't alone. Throughout the tent, girls and women moved gently together. Rachel thought about this as she danced. Where she was from girls never did this. They did it sometimes in private when they were practicing for a party, and very occasionally they might dance fast together in front of boys just to tease, but Rachel had never embraced another girl just for the pleasure of it. Gina seemed entirely comfortable, as if she did it all the time.

Then out of the blue, Grant walked up. She hadn't seen him arrive although she'd been watching for over an hour. Gina broke away; Rachel saw her weaving her way back to the sidelines, to the spot where her sisters and mother stood.

When the dance ended, they walked out, Grant leading her through the swaying crowd, past the band, under the dripping flaps of the tent, and onto the tarmac. A heavy mist had come up from the river making it difficult to see. Grant swept her into the night, his cheek glued to hers, doing a clownish tango step. Sweat streamed from his hairline. She could feel it, cool by the time it reached her, wetting her own brow. She forgot Gina, was blind to everything except the glimmering mists, the lines of sweat on her lover's skin. They moved out of the light, into the private shadows of the tent.

Grant touched her face, her neck, and began to kiss her. They stayed like this for what seemed like hours, clinging to each other like people in a wreck at sea.

When finally they re-emerged into the parking lot—Rachel straightening her shirt and grinning in a crazy, careless way—the music had stopped and many of the cars were gone. They searched for the Grondins, but someone told them they'd left twenty minutes ago or more.

Grant drove her back to Saint Aurélie. When they pulled up in the driveway, the sitting room was glaring like a search light. He left her on the verandah among the empty summer lawn chairs, and she stood for a minute before going in, watching the night swallow his tail lights, gathering courage.

Madame Grondin was sitting by the television in her nightgown. She was alone, and her face was stern and naked with its make-up removed.

"Come and sit," she said when Rachel paused in the hallway.

Rachel was still in her jacket, and the night air followed her into the room. "I'm sorry," she said hurriedly. "I didn't think you'd leave so soon."

"Shh," Madame Grondin said. "The rest of them are asleep." Her face was sad and old-looking in the glare from the television.

"I was with a friend," she said. "I was safe."

"You were with that man again. Look," Madame Grondin said, softening a little. "I don't know how it is in Montreal. Maybe the English let their girls go early. But I'm sure of one thing. He's already a man, Rachel. He'll want things from you."

Rachel couldn't believe Madame Grondin was saying

it. It was private. None of her business. "I'm not a little girl," she blurted. "He'd never push me, and anyways I hate the way it is here." It was out before she could stop herself. She snapped her mouth shut as if she feared she might say more.

Madame Grondin reached for a cigarette, lit it, and the two of them watched smoke curl towards the ceiling, twisting like a vine. Rachel was about to get up when the older woman spoke. "Don't fool yourself, my love." She said it almost to herself, as if she knew Rachel wouldn't listen. "Being with a man doesn't turn you into a woman, just like that. Give yourself time."

Rachel bit her cheeks. Grant Niles seemed to think she was woman enough. What did Madame Grondin know in her little town off in the middle of nowhere? At last she finished her cigarette and let Rachel leave, but it was hours before either of them slept. Rachel heard her in the kitchen as the sky was beginning to lighten.

The love affair between Grant Niles and Rachel was now a public fact. The little Grondin girls and their friends giggled and pointed when they met them in the street. The people in Rachel's class knew. She and Grant inspired heated conversations behind the bread rack in the store, but Rachel had ceased to care. She walked with him openly, sat with him in the leafy graveyard behind the town church, went for drives in his car.

Summer was drawing to a close. The days were cool and windy, and on many nights the sky shimmered with streaks of light. Rachel had never seen the sky move like this before, but Monsieur Grondin explained that it was *un aurore boréal*, the first sign of autumn. Just before their last weekend, Grant suggested a trip. He'd found an island not far from the town with a beach and even a store for provisions.

In the Volkswagon and on the wave-swept shores of the St. Lawrence, she'd grown familiar with Grant's body. She knew the way he moved, how he touched, even what he liked from her. But they'd never had a place where they could be alone. Had Rachel been older it would have been easy to take hotels, leave for whole weekends at a time. But Rachel was just sixteen, and they were living in a place that felt more like an extended family than a town. Privacy was hard to come by.

She let the Grondins know two days before the weekend, in a casual way, through Gina. The Grondins were planning a trip to an uncle's farm, and Gina asked if she were coming.

"No," said Rachel. "Grant Niles is taking me camping." She felt pleased with the way she said it, simply, as if it were the most natural thing in the world.

Gina dropped the cup she was rinsing in the sink and nearly broke it. "Did you tell Maman?"

"Not yet," said Rachel as if it had just crossed her mind. Within an hour the news was out. No one was pleased but this time there were no middle-of-the-night talks. Madame Grondin watched with worried eyes as Rachel ate her dinner at the family table, as she cleaned up with Gina and Marie after the meal.

When Grant arrived on Friday in his beat-up car, no one in the family went out to greet him. Madame Grondin was washing dishes in the kitchen and kept her eyes averted from the window. Grant let the motor run while Rachel went to get her bag. He was like a driver in a bank heist waiting for the chase.

Ile de la Prière was a small farming island right in the

middle of the St. Lawrence River. It was only nine miles long, jutting up out of the water in pastel greens and greys. Looking at it from the shore, Rachel thought of Greek islands and exotic places she'd read about in books. They rented an old trawler which the islanders used to travel back and forth to the mainland. The boatman was starved for company and kept up a steady monologue all the way there. He told them that in winter, the island farmers were completely isolated. Except for the coldest months they couldn't trust the ice with skidoos or cars, so they stayed inside, eating moldy onions and food from cans until the ice was good and solid. The younger men sometimes got impatient and made the trip too soon. It was as if the whiteness swallowed them up, the boatman said. Their bodies would be found months later in the spring thaw, bloated, unidentifiable.

It was cool out on the water even though the sun was shining fiercely. Grant lay on his stomach on the roof of the pilot's cabin and watched Rachel down below on deck. He began to sing old, bawdy drinking songs which Rachel had never heard before. They were very funny, all about stealing kisses and pinching women's behinds.

The beach where the boatman let them off was wild and stretched up one side of the island. The sand was whitish grey and extended back to ragged cliffs of shale. This part of Quebec was a strange mixture of the cultivated and the extremely wild. Orderly fields lay next to cliffs and the cold, churning river. Rachel had never in her life seen land so startling or so beautiful.

They found a sheltered spot and put down their towels. Grant had brought wine and some cheese, and they ate looking out on the water. That afternoon was the most lovely thing that had ever happened to Rachel. She got sleepy and drunk from the wine, and laughed at Grant's jokes and tales of west coast adventures. She couldn't remember ever being so happy. The sun shone down fiercely, and all the wine she'd drunk made the sand glitter and jump. Grant led her down to the shoreline, where the water was dark and so cold it shot slivers of pain through her legs. He took off his bathing suit and knelt down in the waves. Rachel drew in her breath. His buttocks were white, so pale and sculpted, they looked like marble.

Later on, as the sun began to drop and the wine was wearing off, she realized she hadn't brought along warm clothes. It was strange being alone with this man. She felt, all of a sudden, that she barely knew him, and that much of their intimacy had been mere play-acting. They set up a tent on a bed of moss just above the high tide mark. The wind was rising and they were exposed, with no trees or rock to break its force. It was a small tent, held up by string and aluminum poles, with a net door that had to be unzipped before you could crawl in. The nylon walls were red and wind pushed them in bellowing contractions. Lying on the tent floor, Rachel imagined she was trapped inside a live, beating organ.

Grant climbed in. The tent was barely big enough for one and with the wind buffeting its sides they were thrown together, as if someone were shaking them inside a paper bag. Rachel didn't laugh or make small talk. To her embarrassment she went mute and shy as a child. This wasn't necking or touching in the shadows. He was naked in her arms, rubbing against her. She had no voice to tell him it was the first time.

He slept that night, curled like a shell around her. One of his arms was flung across her chest and she lay awake, feeling his weight and listening to waves break against the shore. She was miserable with cold. The sleeping bag was thin and not quite wide enough for two. She thought longingly of the big bed in Saint Aurélie, with the television buzzing down the hall, and the pale Christ watching her as she slept.

The next morning she woke up early. She pulled on her jeans, unzipped the door and climbed out on the rocks. The light was brilliant off the water, and waves exploded in plumes of spray along the shore. It was good to have room again to breathe. The tent was partly collapsed under a weight of dew.

After that weekend, she and Grant didn't have much time. Their few days left were filled with parties, finishing the term's work. The Grondin girls gave her a hand-painted card and told her they loved her. Monsieur Grondin even cried at lunch on the last day after drinking a mug of cognac. Madame Grondin was strangely quiet. She cooked a wonderful meal, steak and onions and fresh tomatoes from the garden, but remained in the background, looking on as her husband and Marie slapped Rachel's back and told jokes they wanted her family back home to hear.

Grant left a few hours before she did. He was driving all the way back to British Columbia and he dropped by the Grondin house on his way to the highway. Rachel rushed into the yard when she saw the car. She was crying and making promises to write, but he just smiled, a little taken aback, and nodded in embarrassment at the family who stood watching through the screen door. After she'd calmed down, he went into the store and shook Monsieur Grondin's hand. He told him it was a long drive and bought fruit and a bottle of water. The little girls and Marie watched him from behind the counter. Their eyes were huge as he paid his bill. Madame Grondin was nowhere to be seen.

Years later, when the name Grant Niles was nothing more than a memory, assimilated long ago into the story of her life, she bumped into him in an airport. It was night and she was dragging her feet with fatigue. They literally tripped over each other in the arrival area. It was clear he recognized her, even though she knew she didn't look at all like the person he'd loved in Saint Aurélie. She was pregnant with her second child and moved awkwardly. He, on the other hand, looked smaller than she remembered, and his hair was fading and thin.

It was in Montreal. Rachel had just arrived home from a conference, and Grant was catching a connecting flight west from overseas. They spoke in English. His voice was nasal and didn't fit at all with her memories. He was still blond, still wore his small military moustache, but he seemed so nervous now. He shifted his feet back and forth and they clicked in their leather boots. He told her he was teaching, unmarried, living in a small town out on Vancouver Island.

Their words began to falter. It was late. He had to find out about departures and Rachel was thinking of home, of the husband and small daughter waiting for her in the city.

As she watched him walk away down the neon airport corridor she remembered Madame Grondin. Perhaps it was the late hour, her exhaustion from being on her feet all day, or maybe the strangeness of seeing a long-buried ghost, but all of a sudden she understood. She hadn't thought of Saint Aurélie for years. It must have been hard for Madame Grondin that summer. She would have known the story only too well; it was such a common plot, so threadbare. But that season in the little coastal town, Rachel couldn't see it. To her, Grant was bigger than life, she couldn't turn away. She thought of what Madame Grondin had tried to tell her. In the middle of Dorval airport, a line from Shakespeare came to her; Cleopatra remembering her first young illusory love.

*My salad days
When I was green in judgement, cold in blood*

There was no way to go back and tell Madame Grondin. She wasn't sure it translated, anyway.

Wing-beat

She wasn't the type of woman to fall into a panic over small things. She was too old for that, had seen too much. She had, for instance, brought four sons into the world and watched them change from tiny, mewling beings to sombre men who towered above her and made weighty pronouncements about government and foreign wars and whether the stock market was likely to dip or rise. She worked in the heart of the city, and even though it was in a library, she managed to see quite a bit. At one time, libraries were protected, quiet places with a predictable clientele. Nowadays you could never tell who would walk in. People with nowhere to sleep warmed themselves in the great, echoing halls on winter afternoons. Downy-haired women flocked together in the stacks and reading areas to lay down for a while their burdens of loneliness. Children wandered in, and people with no money to spare for a newspaper. She wasn't someone who constantly brought fingers to her lips demanding silence. On the contrary, she loved to listen, and over the years, had learned much more from them than from the silent books she stacked each day.

And yet, when she made the discovery that night, stepping from bath to bathmat, her skin a heated rosy shade, she let out a piercing, girlish shriek. In all her years of motherhood and work she had never seen anything like it.

The mirror above the sink was clouded with steam, but even so, she could make them out, shrivelled, black as soot, one sprouting on each shoulder blade. She reached an arm up and poked. The webbing was delicate, fine as the skeletons of leaves and curled inwards at her touch.

A voice came through the bathroom door. It was her youngest son needing to get in. The voice came again, surly this time, impatient. They had one small bathroom which they were forced to share. This was fine for the men in the family. They burst in on each other and shut the doors with two, three of them shaving and bathing all at the same time. She would hear the low humming of their talk mixed with electric razor sounds and splashing. The bathroom was like something you might find at the YMCA. A peculiar, masculine odour of aftershave and sweat hung about it, and no matter how she scrubbed, what quantities of disinfectant she poured over it, the smell remained.

Only her youngest lived with them now. She'd developed a habit of luxuriating in her baths, something she hadn't been able to do for at least twenty-five years. She bought oils and scents and gradually the bathroom had begun to change.

She checked her back again. You really couldn't tell with the robe draped over, unless you knew.

In the beginning, when the bumps first appeared, she thought they were the bites of an insect. She scratched them, wondering that there were two and so evenly spaced, but didn't pay much attention. They swelled. Only this morning they'd grown to the size of small eggs implanted just beneath the skin. Now, in the early evening, they seemed to have transformed into wings, black and webby like those of a bat. She couldn't think what her husband would say. Will was a family doctor and took a great, if somewhat clinical, interest in her body. He prided himself on being observant, his large, manicured hands ferreting out the subtlest changes in her weight, the appearance of pimples, moles, new body hairs. If her latest protrusions had escaped him, it was only because he was suffering from a head cold, and was more than usually tired.

She pushed the bathroom door open a crack and peered out. Her son was no longer waiting, and the house was still. He'd probably left in a fury to shut himself in his room. She walked through the hall, the floor beneath her creaking reassuringly as it had throughout the many years of her marriage.

Her husband was lying on their large green couch. He had swathed his neck with an ascot to comfort his aching glands, and was reading scientific journals, sipping a mug of tea. He didn't look up as she came in.

"How's the throat?" she asked. He made a grunting noise and went on reading. Will wasn't a man who acknowledged illness. It was like giving in, he'd said many times, bowing down to a rebellious, ever-complaining child. "I can make more tea," she tried, but he waved her off, his eyes on the page.

"There's something you must see," she said, and began to loosen her robe. Her husband looked up, then hurried a glance in back of her, checking for sons or other people who might be stalking the corridors at just that moment. The robe slipped down around her shoulders and she gathered it about her like a cape. Then she knelt beside the sofa, baring her back and neck.

"What is it?" he whispered, and dry, tentative fingers began to palpate her.

Doctor with the healing hands. It had been a while

since they'd touched. She pictured the long fingers with their groomed nails rubbed and sanded so as not to catch, the whites at their base peering up like tired moons. He poked and prodded, fingering the webbing while she crouched patiently, her skin cooling in the night air. They stayed like this a long while, and he seemed to have forgotten her when finally, in a voice much lower and graver than his own, he asked when the warts had first pushed through.

Warts. That was the word he used.

Later that night, she heard him talking on the phone. He whispered so as not to upset her, but his voice was raspy, coarse from the head cold, and she heard the words *tumour*, *malignancy*. Much later, when they were in bed, he made her lie on her side, the warts, limp now and folded, facing him. "I'll keep an eye on them," he said, the doctor with his patient, and made no move to embrace her before sleep carried her off.

She awoke to sun flooding through their thin rice paper blind and the sensation that someone was watching her, and without thinking, rolled over on her back.

"You've crushed them!" she heard, and then saw Will's wide eyes. He made her sit on the bed with sheets and blankets strewn around them and examined her, kneeling behind her out of sight so that only through her skin could she sense what he was doing. Again the fingers prodded, traced the contours of blades, ribs, spinal column, deftly, softly.

"They grew in the night," he said finally. "Today they're horny, like a reptile's skin."

He described how mysterious warts could be. How they could spring up for no reason it seemed, at any age, without warning. How the roots often went very deep, and how difficult they were to remove. He used long Latin words and spoke of ablation, and of using nitroglycerine to blast down to the wart's core. She tried to follow what he was saying, but she couldn't see him and without seeing him, she couldn't concentrate.

A wave of self-disgust washed through her. Will was frightened. He used the calm, even tones that he reserved for his most hopeless cases at work. He could do this, separate the scientific from the human. If she were the doctor, she'd constantly be crying with people, touching them, unable to stem the pain that would overtake her in the most common, unprofessional way. Will knew this. He said it was the one great difference between them. He was disciplined, she was emotional and rather scattered. Even in a library, which he imagined to be the driest and dullest of places, he was struck by how she sniffed out and found the hints of pain.

Black warts on her back. How could he even touch her? She imagined long, hair-like roots winding through her ribs, stretching tentacles out to clasp soft, hidden organs.

Will was behind her, poking at her back, his voice floating up in waves in the light-filled room. In the patches of silence between each of her husband's observations, her mind began to wander. She thought of a strange, very involving dream she'd dreamt at dawn, just before waking. It seemed so real that she lay there exhausted for many minutes, unable to move, aching from the night's exertions.

The air was like water and she was running through it down hills of yellow grass. The hills were not steep, but big enough to give her momentum, and she moved her arms in front of her in slow arcs like a swimmer. At the base of one of the hills her feet lifted from the ground. It was so unexpected, yet familiar somehow, as if she'd done it often long ago, in a life only dimly remembered. Her clumsy limbs were weightless now, like balloons only more graceful, more purposeful against the wind. She was no longer running but gliding low in the air, pulling herself along with an odd, breast-stroking motion. At first the flight was uneven. She dipped and rose like a kite on a string, but she pulled hard and climbed until she could coast on gusts of wind. Gravity stopped at the tops of trees, and above this the air currents were strong. Wind and her own momentum propelled her, and she looked down at the shrinking earth with a strange calm and wonder.

Will's voice brought her back to earth. He was in front of her looking very glum, talking about contagion.

"I had the strangest dream," she said, thinking that perhaps it was the one bright spot in this whole affair, that it might distract him for a moment. But Will just stared as if she didn't see the point at all. He continued where he left off before she interrupted. She must phone in sick, rest as much as she could until they decided what to do. One of his colleagues, a man called Brais whom she vaguely remembered from a hospital party, would have a look at her. They needed a surgeon's opinion, and no one was more qualified in all the city than Brais.

She nodded listlessly. Will was taking charge. He was rallying forces where she would have scattered them. He'd figure things out; it would be all right. But strangely, deep in her heart, she didn't care. She couldn't summon the energy even to worry. Her limbs were almost melting into the bedsheets and she was heavy, too worn out to move.

Doctor Brais's office was on the top floor of the sprawling, new hospital complex where Will worked. He was a nervous, tall young man whose mouth wasn't wide enough to stretch into a smile. His eyes seemed to take in her body in a single glance, filing details for future deliberations. He was ill at ease with Will standing in the corner, observing. Will had insisted on attending the examination. He'd never seen warts shaped like wings before, and hadn't found anything even remotely resembling them in his medical books. He presented her to Brais as a prize specimen to which he had at least a partial claim.

She hunched forward on the table, cradling her breasts. It was strange to be sitting there half naked in front of the men. Sometimes when she was in a doctor's office, she forgot about her body. It became extraneous, like a coat that could be tossed aside and studied quite impassively. She and the doctor would discuss the body together, as if her thoughts were something apart from the carcass on the table. But with her husband there, she couldn't manage it. She saw her breasts through his eyes, as flesh that had given him pleasure, that he'd seen alter with the years, that had brought his sons their first rich tastes of love and life. She was ashamed to expose this intimacy before another man. She knew she looked old. Fleshy, lumpy, with wide stretch marks down her front. For this too, she was ashamed. She must look helpless with Brais behind her, poking at the wings, turning her this way and that, pushing her arms out and back to determine whether her shoulders and arms had been affected.

She thought again of her dream. In sleep she must have felt the warts and transformed them into wings. Whatever inspired it, the images were striking today. When she shut her eyes a vision of herself, weightless, soaring high above trees appeared as if it had been burnt into each retina.

After the examination, she spent two hours with hospital technicians who worked on her with dogged efficiency. Her husband had to leave for work and Brais remained in his office, so she was alone with the men in white laboratory coats, who ordered her to strip from the waist up, who photographed her, x-rayed her, extracted blood and urine samples, gave her forms to fill out on allergies and diseases in her family line, on whether she had ever, to her knowledge, been exposed to high levels of radiation. Damp hands kneaded her back, touching her only when necessary, to examine how the warts were grafted to the skin or to perfect an angle for a photograph. She abandoned herself to them, hardly paying attention until, without warning her, they clipped off the tips of each wart, dabbed the stinging blood with cotton, and placed the amputated bits into a large and clearly-labelled envelope.

She was stunned when she saw the small black pieces. One of the technicians held them up to the light between the prongs of a pair of tweezers and all of a sudden she was outraged. She hadn't known cutting would be necessary. No one had consulted her or even mentioned this might happen. Perhaps, she thought, she hadn't until then had strong feelings either way. Perhaps Will and the expert Doctor Brais had assumed quiescence because she'd shown nothing else. The amputation jolted her awake. It was her skin the warts had chosen. Her body Brais would blast into to get at the roots. The warts were part of her. She jumped up from the bench and left the men in the lab coats standing in a consultative circle around the tweezers, watching her as if she were a madwoman. She hurried out, hair flying, clutching her half-buttoned blouse to her chest.

When she reached the house, the front hall was dark and empty, and she went straight for the bathroom. She was completely exhausted, grimy with the contact of so many hands. Her torso was wrapped with long strips of gauze, above and below her breasts, and she looked something like a buried Egyptian queen who had started to unravel. She unwrapped herself delicately with all the tenderness she could muster after the hospital, and her body began to emerge, soft, vulnerable from under the bandages. As the last strip came off, she heard rustling. Something fell to the floor and she jumped away from it, off the bathmat, thinking with a mixture of relief and fear that it must be a wart dropping. Perhaps they were deciduous, like leaves or the horns of deer. Or maybe the taping had damaged them, cut off the blood supply or broken their fragile cores. It was too small for a wing and too light. She swivelled to the mirror and, for the second time in her long life, screamed like a schoolgirl.

The warts had grown. They were now as big as the wings of a blackbird and feathers had sprouted. This was the black that had fallen; she was molting. The warts were so different now. When she first discovered them there had been something repulsive about them. Their webbiness and the suggestion of reptiles had filled her with ambivalence. But they now looked almost beautiful. She reached to stroke them with a tenderness and care she hadn't felt since her sons were small. They were so different from the bat's wings, covered with a blanket of blue-black plumes and gleaming like some precious stone, even in the dull bathroom light.

She was in the bathtub experimenting with her new body when Will returned. The wings were far more solid than they looked. Their feathers were waterproof, and she dipped them in the water, much like birds did in the park, and gently flapped them dry. She had no trouble flapping. It was as if she had two sets of arms, one at each side and one invisible in back which she could move or shake with ease. She was waving one wing in regular beats, holding the other perfectly still, when Will walked in.

"Look at me!" she said, and gave a playful splash.

Will's face, normally stern, expressive, turned strangely soft when he saw her, with a hint of grey like uncooked dough.

That night, with her husband dutifully watching her backside, she dreamed again of wings. The dream came easily the moment she shut her eyes, as if it had been hovering somewhere near all through the day. She grew daring as the night wore on, gliding high above the trees, flipping upside down, like a looping daredevil pilot, engraving her name on a cloudless sky.

In the morning she was exhausted, her limbs so heavy she couldn't stir from bed. The wings had grown again and were now speckled with white, like those of a young sea gull. Will, his face even greyer than the night before, made frenzied phone calls, then hurried from the house as if it were on fire. "We'll do something," he told her, trying to convince them both that things were still under control, that he, the doctor, was in charge. He left promising to arrange things, to call her from the hospital.

When finally she pulled herself from the bed she was startled at the change in her. She had somehow grown terribly thin. Ribs jutted out from her sides and her breasts drooped sadly. She felt faint and vertiginous and staggered when she tried to walk. Her centre of gravity had shifted. Her body was wasting away and all the time the wings were growing, sucking the life right out of her.

She climbed back into bed and lay on her side, fetally, tucking her wings in so as not to disturb the feathers. Beside her a window was open and the sounds of a city morning filled the room. Rush of tires on wet pavement, the intermittent blasts of horns. On days like this in early summer, the green of trees was startling. It had something to do with the clouds. When the clouds were low and the sun was strong behind them, the colour of the city changed. Greens that most days blended uncomplainingly with the backdrop wash of sky, sprang out sharply. They were doing this today. She couldn't take her eyes off them. Branches heavy with green waved to her softly, a hair's breadth away.

She felt very sad and tired. Obviously she couldn't go on like this. Her dreams had taken over, invading her each night, sweeping her away. She'd aged, lost weight. Each morning it was as if years had passed. She was obsessed with the dizzying, spiralling feeling of flight. It filled her at night and now, during the day, her mind returned to it again and again. It was bleeding her, sapping her strength. Her ordinary daytime life was so different, so irreconcilable with it. She couldn't think what would become of her if the wings continued to grow, if her dreams continued.

The house was empty. She could relax for a few hours. When Will or her son was there she felt like an invalid, like something maimed, deformed. Alone in her bed it was better. She could linger over her dreams, call back the heady, tumbling flight. She slipped her hand under the sheets and fingered the soft, oiled feathers.

Will arrived home to find her crouched on her knees, exhausted, pale as stone and letting out thin moans. Her wings were enormous, pewter-coloured like a heron's, like the wings of a Dürer angel. He threw himself to her side, weeping, mumbling words of comfort. Everything was taken care of. There was a room reserved for her the next day, and Brais promised to work on her first thing in the morning.

She nodded vaguely, knowing he loved her, that he was trying to reach her, but she felt so sleepy, so unutterably exhausted. The lids of her eyes closed and she couldn't find energy to open them again. Will's words came to her in gusts, as if he were walking away across an immense, windswept plain.

The first thing she heard was singing. She must have been asleep. All around her voices echoed, reverberating through the thick, blanketed woods. Light filtered through clutches of leaves, dancing on rough bark surfaces, or crept lower to warm the steaming, damp, black earth.

She must have left through the window. She couldn't recall. Somehow she'd come to this place filled with singing, winged creatures who watched her now from the surrounding trees. She no longer had a body. She was all bird—sleek, whitish-grey with immense wings, talons sharp enough to cut through flesh.

She knew somehow that this was no dream. She would end her days here, never return to her home in the city. It didn't sadden her. Perhaps sadness never occurred to birds. And although her memory eventually grew dim, she never entirely forgot Will, or her sons, or her life as a woman. Each day she rose early with the sun, half hoping, wondering if Will would ever think to look for her in the leafy, overgrown ravine.

This Really Isn't It

Sun was seeping through cracks in the shutters, and a steady rhythmic thumping pushed Mavis into consciousness. She rolled over, not yet disengaged from her dream. For several seconds she couldn't imagine where she was or where the drummers were hiding. In her dream, she'd been in the jungle. The drum beats were signals, greetings sent to her across miles of dense green forest.

She'd overslept again. Slept right through Réal's getting up, the flush of the toilet and the rushing sound of water. She'd slept through his pulling things from the closet, the hangers jangling and jumping, his creaking down the hall, the kitchen sounds, smell of Turkish coffee, syrupy and black as tar, and, at roughly half past eight, the noise of his key in the lock. All through September she'd awakened with the sun high in the sky, alone in his bed. At night they didn't sleep until the sky began to glimmer and lighten. They haunted cafés, wandered through the different quarters or else stayed in and read, listened to his tapes and to some new ones she'd added to the collection. Sometimes Jasmine dropped by, or José and Françoise, who was seven months pregnant, and they spent the evening talking. Mavis always tried to make them stay.

She pulled on one of Réal's shirts and wandered to the

bathroom. She was tawny and lean, her straight blondish hair bleached and whitened by summer. Paris sun could not have done this, it so rarely showed its drawn face; Crete and the Aegean were responsible. Mavis and Réal had spent July touring Greece and then returned to an empty, overcast Paris in August.

She fastened the buttons on his shirt. He really was a big man. The shirt was tight on him, on her it flapped like an overcoat. She was tall for a woman and also slender. The streets of American and Canadian cities were filled with girls who looked like her— angular, boyish, plainly-dressed. In Paris, she stood out. She towered above most women and heads turned as she walked down the dim streets with her long, masculine strides. Réal found her exotic, like the tanned and light-haired beauties in Hollywood films.

Mavis, on her side, loved Réal's foreignness. He was French-speaking and Jewish, originally from Tunisia, and unlike any man she had ever met. He certainly was different from the ones she met at parties, in cafés and cinema lineups all over Paris. Réal was bigger, for one thing, muscled and heavy. His skin had the inevitable urban pallor, but his hair was wiry, longish and solidly black. He had none of the arrogance which had disturbed her so much when she first arrived. Réal was a listener; he also loved to laugh.

She splashed water on her face and rubbed her eyes. Her tan had faded to a diluted mustard colour. Soon there would be no trace left. She took a crayon from her half of the medicine cabinet and drew blue lines around each eye. The irises shone out like limpid seas. Better, she thought. A touch here, a touch there. It wasn't so bad.

In the kitchen Réal had left out bread and a pat of sweet butter. She'd never gotten used to this delicacy, preferring the cruder salty stuff of everyday America. Réal marvelled at her tastes. The French liked sauces and pulpy things that didn't demand much of the teeth. Mavis loved to chew. She liked things raw and grainy with simple, bold strokes of flavour. She missed foods from home. Recently she had developed the habit of eating halva candy as a kind of ersatz peanut butter spread on slices of brown *complet* from the corner baker. Parisians disdained brown bread. Even Réal was a purist.

The table was covered with crumbs. Mavis swept these into a pile and deposited them in the sink. Then she rinsed out the little metal coffee pot and filled it with water. Outside the kitchen window a woman was pounding away on her rugs. Clouds of dust hovered weightlessly in the soft morning light. The sound was comforting with its steady beat, but also disturbing. It broke the customary stillness of the courtyard.

She sat down with a half-full cup of coffee and pulled an envelope out from underneath the butter dish. It was torn and soiled with grease, but the backwards slanting hand was unmistakable. It was the first letter she'd had from Hal in two months, ever since her announcement that she wouldn't be going home. He was furious with her, she knew that, but distance muted his fury, robbed it of its power. She was safe with the Atlantic tossing cold and grey between them.

The tone of the letter wasn't angry. This surprised her. Hal was a busy man and he didn't look well on anyone, least of all his own daughter, throwing away precious days of her life. Two months ago, just after she'd returned from Greece, his voice had come across the wires, crackling, tight, sarcastic. The letter was different, calmer, asking about Réal, about her life with him. There were fragments of news about her sisters and a scribbled line from her mother, who wrote every couple of weeks in a hurried hand to remind her that Hal was sick with worry and that in any event she had to make up her mind, sooner or later, as to what she wanted to do with her life.

But Hal's letter, this first message, had a tone she didn't recognize. A ring of sadness, almost of unsureness.

She hadn't written for a while now. Montreal, her family, her life of a year ago seemed impossibly distant. She had trouble making the link between this new Paris Mavis she had become and the younger, less worldly, more timid Mavis of the past. In Paris she spoke French, not the dull American English of her home. She'd moved in with a man for the first time after her term at the Sorbonne had ended. She spent her days exploring odd corners of the city, chatting with people in cafés, reading de Beauvoir and Gertrude Stein.

When she first met Réal, she talked incessantly of Montreal. She described the stone house where her parents lived in the English section, half way up a mountain. Montreal had two mountains. They were not really mountains, she explained, not compared to the Alps or the Pyrenées, but Montrealers called them this out of pride or perhaps out of ignorance. She told of the river, the inky black water choked with debris and weeds. If you followed it east there were cliffs and then the water turned salt and so blue and cold that whales came down from the Arctic. She told of snow and savage winds that kept children inside entire days in winter; of the breathless heat of summer. Réal had a vivid impression of her home. One time he told her she was like her city, a mingling of odd and startling contrasts. As the months rolled by and she settled into Paris, Mavis spoke less of Montreal, thought less about the past. Her sense of her home, her family, the Mavis she had been only the previous year grew somehow dimmer, like a dream fading as daylight pushes into a room.

She was supposed to meet Réal at noon. Mavis jumped up, still holding the letter, and ran to find a watch. It was almost eleven. Not worth eating breakfast. She knotted her hair into a loose chignon and slipped into a skirt and sweater. The days were less warm now, less predictable. In a Paris autumn, the cold crept in slowly. September and October were filled with sultry, gentle days, but Mavis, who came from a climate which shifted violently with little warning, dressed warmly, sensing change in the air.

The café where they had arranged to meet had a large stepped terrace that swept up like a bandstand from the street. Americans liked to sit out over the broad avenues and watch the crowds pass by. Few Parisians used these tables. They preferred to stand at the bar in the dusky gloom of the interior, even at midday, where coffee was cheaper and they could chat with the waiters. The terrace tables would come in soon, as soon as summer was indisputably over, but the café owners liked to keep them out as long as they could. They were like well-practiced hosts flattering a guest, cajoling, trying to convince the soft season that it should stay a while longer.

Mavis chose a table three rows up from the street and off to one side. The rest of the terrace was empty save for a table to her left with a young couple and a baby. The woman was chattering away in a familiar English. She and her husband could have been twins in their khaki shorts, flat sandals and sweatshirts. Even the child was in a sweatshirt. Bubblegum pink, and she was tearing apart a steaming croissant. Eastern seaboard, Mavis thought. New York, Pennsylvania, one of those states. The waiter was with them and they were trying to order milk for the child. The woman kept saying *leche, leche,* as if she could not keep straight what country she was in.

Mavis straightened her skirt. These days she wouldn't be caught dead in shorts and sweatshirts. It was as bad as draping oneself in a flag with the word *America* painted all over it. When the waiter came to take her order, impatient, unsmiling, expecting perhaps that he would have to translate the menu or listen to a tortured and broken variant of his native tongue, Mavis opened her mouth and asked for an *alongé* in a clipped, musical and near perfect French. She could feel the couple watching.

Réal was on the pavement, waving to her. He took the stairs two at a time up to her table. He was beautiful. It always startled her to see him at a distance. He was so dark, such a big man. At times like this she had to remind herself as if she were appreciating it for the first time, that this was Réal, her Réal of Paris, that he was hers, that they were linked and shared a world here. He came up to the table flushed, breathing hard, and hugged her. The waiter floated up from somewhere behind and smiled at Réal saying that they had picked the last nice day of the season to dine out of doors, while Réal ordered lavishly, carelessly, without looking at the menu, knowing her tastes.

"This day reminds me of Greece. Of holidays," he said, reaching under the table and stroking her thigh. "God how I wish I had days free to spend with you."

"You'd have to spend them in bed," Mavis said. "I've turned into such a sleeper. I sleep and sleep while you're at work." She remembered the drums that had awakened her that morning. In Paris she dreamed constantly and very vividly. But then, it made sense she should be so aware of dreams. What was her life now but longer and longer stretches of sleep?

"I'd make sure you wouldn't sleep. You need me for

a cure." Réal laughed and slipped off his jacket. His shirt and pants were white and he looked striking, like an Arab, stretching back in his chair. "Tonight we are seeing Dezzy and Jacob," he said. "You hadn't forgotten?"

Dezzy and Jacob were his parents. Réal was in his early thirties, more than a decade older than she was. The boys in his family had been brought up in Tunisia but had come to the University of Paris to study. Réal, the baby, was a journalist. Five years before, he'd brought his parents across the sea to start a new life. Those were difficult times for Jews in Tunisia. One evening Jacob's business was gutted by bombs, and three days later a cousin was killed. Jacob and Dezzy dropped everything they had, the business, the houses, their friends, their books and paintings, and smuggled themselves out of the country to Paris.

"I knew. Is this skirt okay?" she said.

"Anything you do is *okay*," he said, mimicking the way she lingered over vowels. "Dezzy and Jacob love you. You could go naked and we'd still be happy. Happier even."

"They'd think I was just being foreign," she said and began to eat a salad which the waiter had laid down.

"They're happy that I'm happy," Réal said. "But more than that, they love you. They know I've got good taste."

"Did you see I got a letter from home?" Mavis said. "My father," she added when he shook his head. "He has a birthday in October, soon in fact. It's the second year I'm missing it."

Réal couldn't stay more than an hour. He kissed her, settled the bill and ran off to find his beat up Renault, which he usually parked in alleyways or in the yards of schools or churches. Mavis, left with her glass of wine and some coffee, watched him hurry away. As he ran he struggled to put on his jacket, which was dull grey and nondescript, and blended easily with the other jackets of office clerks on the street. She cleared the round marble table top, piling plates, the bread basket, the ashtray and Réal's wineglass on the table next to hers. The American couple were getting up from their seats and climbing down the cluttered stairs to the street. The woman had slung the child on her back, papoose-style, and they looked vaguely like pioneers setting off. Now the terrace was completely empty. She reached into her purse and pulled out a card that she had bought the day before, just after receiving Hal's letter. It was royal blue. A blue sea with a pair of carmine lips curling into a smile, floating in its middle like a boat. A diminutive inky man with a gondolier's pole stood on the underlip patiently pushing his way through the water.

She took out her old fountain pen and shut her eyes. What could she say? Her Paris life was sleep. She had nothing to show, nothing to tell. She was just living. Marking time in the endless tugging forward that was life. She wished she could send the blank card, which was exquisite and perfect, and forget about words.

She stared at the floating lips and finally, without even removing the cap from her pen, inserted the card back into its envelope and slipped it into a pocket of her skirt. She would wait until the words came.

"You mustn't say a word about how thin he is getting," Réal whispered in the elevator. "He's very sensitive about it."

Mavis nodded. Over the last months she'd come to love Jacob and to understand his humours and his moods. "He's proud, your father," she whispered back. "It's good. At his age so many lose it."

The door to the apartment was partly open and a warm

smell of chicken filled the corridor. Réal poked his head inside. "Dezzy?" he called. His mother came running from the kitchen holding a wooden spoon, a great lopsided smile on her face.

She stopped before them and beamed as if she couldn't quite believe it. "Jacob!" she cried. "Jacob, come! Your son is here." Réal bent to kiss her. In his parents' apartment he was enormous. The top of his head grazed Dezzy's low ceilings. Her cluttered rooms barely held him. They stood waiting silently until Jacob joined them. She was like that, always deferring to the men in the family. Jacob was so much frailer than she and twenty years older, but even so she spent her days in his shadow.

They went into the front room, which served as living- and dining-room both, and sat down. Dezzy had dragged a round table out from its usual spot in the corner. It was the Sabbath and the wine and spices and bread were already laid out. Dezzy never sat before the meal. She shuffled back and forth carrying things, mixing, basting, preparing. They had a while to wait until sundown. Réal settled on the worn couch beside Mavis. He stretched his big arms out behind her and his long legs under the table, and all at once the apartment seemed to contract. Jacob sat on a swivel chair and smiled at them. "Dezzy," he shouted, "they need drinks. And something to stave off an appetite."

Dezzy appeared with beads of perspiration gleaming like gems on her forehead. "Fish," she said loudly. "Does she like fish?" *Fish* was Dezzy's word for a salty, blood-red caviar that the family brought in from North Africa. Mavis and Réal ate it often. It came in a solid roll and you cut it with a knife. Mavis nodded her head vigorously. "Fish! She likes fish!" Dezzy said, laughing, and ran off to the kitchen. She returned minutes later with a heavy tray. She had mixed cloudy glasses of anise. There were plates with roasted cashews, fish and drooping artichokes with a dish of liquid yellow butter.

"This is dinner in itself," Mavis said but Dezzy had already disappeared.

"It's your second autumn here," Jacob said. "It must be almost like home now."

Mavis nodded. Jacob was a frail, shrunken man. The hands folded on his lap were spotted. Veins streaked them a dirty blue. "Autumn here is lovely," she said. "It's softer than in Montreal. It sneaks up more slowly. Back home it's a sudden burst of colour. Then winter comes and covers everything in white."

"What's the name of that tree?" Réal asked. "The one that gives sugar?"

"That's cane you're thinking of, from the south," Jacob said.

"No," said Mavis. "In Canada there is a tree that gives a strong, very sweet sugar every spring. In autumn its leaves blaze like fire. *L'erable,*" she pronounced.

"A tree that gives sugar, whose green leaves turn red. You're teaching things to an old man," Jacob said and laughed.

"You'd recognize it," Réal said. "It's on their flag. You've seen it, I'm sure." He turned to Mavis. "Why don't you draw it?"

Mavis took a pen out of her purse and began an outline on one of Dezzy's napkins. What she drew was roundish, lopsided, with tiny toothlike notches carved into its sides. "This isn't really it," she said, putting on the final touches. The leaf grinned like a spikey gourd and Mavis realized she'd never looked at a maple leaf close up.

Jacob came and stood behind her. "I don't know this," he said, shrugging. "Looks like a cactus, or maybe one of those." He pointed at a soggy artichoke lying in a puddle of greenish water.

Dezzy came in then to say the food was ready. "We are speaking of leaves," Jacob told her, and she smiled as she would have smiled if he'd said philosophy or love or life or death. Talking was outside her arena. It was for men and for the modern girls her sons brought home to dinner. This was so different from Mavis's home. Mavis came from a family of women, four daughters who loved to talk and argue and jostle for attention. Dinners were a free-for-all with many voices trying out opinions, talking of styles and politics, of movie stars, the weather, books read, conversations overheard on buses. Women in her family were strong and very voluble. "You should take Réal to Canada," Jacob said. The smile dropped from Dezzy's face and she stared at her husband. "To visit," Jacob added. "To see the trees with the marvellous colours."

They stood at their places at the table while Jacob began the blessings. Mavis had become adept at the Sabbath rituals. She could recite most of the prayers in Hebrew even though she didn't know what they meant. Jacob took a silver goblet filled to the brim with wine and said the *borucha*. He drank long and noisily and then passed the cup to his son, who did the same. The cup was passed to Dezzy, and finally to Mavis, who stumbled through the prayer with Réal's help. "Your fiancée is very good!" Dezzy cried when Mavis had finished. Réal looked at his mother aghast, and Mavis flushed red as the wine she had just brought to her lips. She and Réal hadn't spoken of marriage. Not once.

Jacob blessed the bread, dipped it in salt and handed it

around. Then they sat down to dinner. Dezzy ladled out two immense helpings of *couscous* and boiled chicken. She and Jacob had to be content with a greasy yellow broth. Once during the meal, he reached out for a slice of caviar, but Dezzy slapped his hand back with the end of her spoon. "He gets so tired of the diet," she sighed to no one in particular.

Mavis nibbled at the steaming mountain on her plate. The food was insipid, bulky. Réal was making a mighty effort to plough through his. It pleased Dezzy so much to watch him eat. Mavis thought of her own mother back in Montreal, a sharp-eyed, intense woman. Her mother often argued with Hal, with her daughters, just for the fun of it. She was irreverent. Odd, unexpected things came out of her mouth. She thought of Hal, aging master of their house, the only male. It seemed to Mavis that the women engaged in a continuous ritualistic dance about him, like planets rotating about a sun. There was an unspoken pact that he was the focus of attention, and no male child had come to upset this delicate system. To be fair, Hal adored women. Perhaps the sheer force of numbers had drawn respect out of him.

Mavis put her spoon down. Réal and his father were talking about Israel, its inflation and violence. "In spite of it all," Jacob was saying, "it's still God's country. The most beautiful spot ..." She stopped listening. She could do this with French. English always managed to filter through, regardless of the lengths she went to tune it out, but French she could turn off. Réal's voice faded to a hum, a backdrop for her thoughts.

What was she doing here in Paris, eating strange food, describing maple trees and Quebec autumns to people who would never know them? Dezzy was beginning to regard her as a daughter. Jacob spoke of Paris as her home. Yet Paris was so foreign. And Dezzy and Jacob would never be family. For the first time in months, her thoughts turned to Hal and to Montreal.

In the street Réal took her in his arms. "They're crazy about you," he said, nuzzling the top of her head.
    "They're crazy about *you*," she answered, but she was no longer really with him. Her mind was on her father, on a sapphire sea and the words she'd chosen to tell him that she was coming home.

Jyoti

It suddenly dawned on Candice that someone was calling her. Two boys kneeling by a trench were grinning and waving their hands wildly in the air. After four months in Guyana, she still jumped when students called out to her. They called her "Miss," and it made her feel like laughing, like pulling faces and shouting that she was barely out of school herself, too young, too ordinary for such a precious name.

She waved across the weeds at them. Sun flooded the road, turning the dust at her feet a startling gold. She walked quickly towards the centre of town, a book by V.S. Naipaul clutched under one arm. Today had not been good. She'd been reading aloud to her class, something she was forced to do often because the school owned so few books, and she'd read *l.b.w.* as "pound weight", a term that must have come percolating up from some long-forgotten physics class. The boys had stared at her, then roared with delight. What a blunder. What an unforgiveable, alien blunder. The girls had been indignant, defending her in shrill voices.

"She from Canada, man. It not every person care about cricket. Stupid game is all."

The street narrowed and a sharp smell of burnt wood and manure came to her. A house was being built here, its yard full of stone and fresh cut timber. She inhaled, trying to keep the smell with her, to decipher it.

Up ahead was the worst part of the walk. The rum shop. Men slouched in the shade of the doorway, drinking beer and cheap liquor.

"You der!" A very thin man staggered into the street. Candice hunched forward. "You der!" the man called again. She was almost even with the shop's gate, body tense, ready to break and run. "You na hear me, girl?"

Laughter erupted from the rum shop porch as the man stopped before her, swaying, arms outstretched. "Leave she be, man," someone yelled and then, all at once, the skies seemed to open. Whistles, catcalls rained down upon her, ricocheted through yards, split the stillness of the afternoon. Candice dodged the thin man who blocked her way, and broke into a sprint. Knees high, V.S. Naipaul pumping up and down, up and down to give her speed. What would they think, these men? Guyanese women never ran. Always kept their cool. Used their tongues and torrents of words to keep the men off. She would never learn. She wasn't even that pretty. Long, spidery limbs, hair in a braid. In their eyes she must look like an oversized schoolgirl. But she was white, and that seemed enough to interest the men at the rum shop.

Finally she made it to the Singhs' street, where she was staying for the term. The wire gate was swinging on its rusty hinges, welcoming her into the overgrown yard filled with rows of yellowed sheets hung out to dry. A chorus of sitars whined piteously, like crickets. Jyoti was home from work. Candice could always tell from the music when Jyoti was around.

Jyoti's hair was smudged with flour and her hands were plunged deep into a bowl of dough which she was pressing, kneading into a dull, greyish ball. She looked up at

Candice and then back down at the dough. Her face was serious as a child's, fat lips pouting.

"Roti?" Candice asked.

Jyoti nodded, still sombre, then ducked past Candice to change a tape. She sometimes moved like that, like an animal, like something wild. It was because of Blackburn. Jyoti had been raised out on the coast. Once she had told Candice all about her childhood. About rice flats stretching for mile after mud-black mile between the water ditches. As a child she'd had the run of the fields, swum in long, glassy trenches, driven donkeys to help her father at harvest time. Now her nails were painted, her feet jammed into clumsy platform shoes. But every once in a while, when she was tired or private in her home, she moved like that, fluid, beautiful.

Jyoti shook her hair so that it fell about her in a cloak of loose and careless curls, and turned up the volume. The sitars whined louder now, like cats. "Lord," she sighed, her voice rising and losing itself in the music, and burst into tears.

For many days Jyoti, or Judith as they called her at work, had been mooning about, missing meals, showing up hours after her shift at work had ended. Nathan had no patience for the girl. She was his youngest sister, moved down from the countryside to help with his son, Ravi, and with chores after his wife died. He had no time for her moods. He needed a woman in the house, not a second child. One night after she let a stew boil dry, he started screaming. "Jyoti girl. You na good!" He sucked hard on his teeth. "All you good for is to play dos tapes. You not wort de groun you mother walk on."

Jyoti turned to Candice, making a nervous, birdlike motion with her arms. She tried to speak, choked, began again, gulping air. "Me na bleed dis month, Candice. Oh God, me na bleed."

At first Candice couldn't make her out. Sitars and tears blurred her words. Finally it hit her. Jyoti was pregnant. She was saying that she was pregnant.

Candice said nothing for several seconds and just stared at Jyoti. The girl was so young. Candice had to keep reminding herself that she was twenty, just a year younger than Candice was herself. She had no life of her own outside of the Singh house. She never went anywhere, except to work, without Nathan or Ravi. She still had girlfriends from high school whom she visited very occasionally with Nathan's permission, but in all the weeks Candice had lived with her, there hadn't been even a whisper about a man.

"De man who done it na be good," Jyoti sobbed. "Him sweetboy. Talk sweet to all de girl."

Candice knew him vaguely. She'd seen him at the market leaning over a stall for sunglasses. He was a heavy set man, and not particularly attractive. Candice tried to picture small, round-faced Jyoti embracing him.

Several weeks ago when Candice and Jyoti had cycled past the sports club, he had slipped out to greet them. Jyoti, perched on the back carrier, had begged Candice to stop. The merchant, who looked as if he had just woken up, with a ragged beard and sleepy, large-lidded eyes, had reached into a pocket and pulled out a tape, neatly wrapped in plastic with a Bombay film star singing on the front. Jyoti had held out both hands, laughing.

"He's older," Candice said. "Married."

Jyoti's face darkened, swelled like a sponge in water. She threw herself on Candice's neck and wailed, "Natan, he goin to kill me."

Candice tried to quiet her. She wondered why Jyoti

was telling her, the white woman. She wondered if the merchant knew.

The front door banged. Jyoti fled to the back porch just as Ravi came in, his jacket streaked with dust, blood caked on his lip. "You cookin?" he said casually to Candice. "Where be Judit?"

He launched into a complicated story about a fight he'd won at school. "Dat fatboy, dat Balky. Tink he some great gif to dis earth jus because he fadder a lawyer." In Creole, lawyers were called liars, and Ravi loved the pun. "He so stupid and proud dat one."

Then Ravi remembered his aunt again. "But where be Judit? She wash dis before my fadder get home and get vex." Candice tried to distract him, but the porch door opened. Jyoti stood framed in the doorway, her hair wild and powdered white. Ravi puffed his chest. "What you mean bein outside?" he asked in a harsh voice, sensing that something was very wrong. Jyoti's eyes were full of hatred. "You so smart wit all you secrets. Up to no good, girl, I sure of it."

They waited three more days before doing anything. Candice came home early after school to help with the chores. Jyoti seemed drugged with fear. She wasn't eating, and Candice would find her sitting in her room in silence, staring at nothing. The house was sombre and still.

Jyoti didn't want anyone to know, not Nathan, not her family, no friend, not even the merchant. She begged Candice not to tell. Her life was over, she said. Her only hope was to get rid of the child in secret. Candice tried to comfort her, but in bed alone at night, she cried and felt very lost. Jyoti knew next to nothing about sex, about how to care for her body or protect it. She'd never been taught. Now there was a child inside her. She'd pay heavily for innocence.

On the fourth day, Candice and Jyoti walked in the hard sunlight to the office of Doctor Malik. The doctor's gate, fronting a makeshift verandah waiting room, was blistered and peeling. Beyond it at least twenty women crouched, some alone and wretched-looking, others big-bellied and smiling, accompanied by chattering female family. Jyoti shrank under their eyes. She sat at the edge of the verandah and stared at cloud banks gathering for the afternoon rain. Over an hour later her name was called by a large woman with blue eyes and skin as milky as Candice's.

Jyoti sat in a hard-backed wicker chair while the woman questioned her. "Name?"

"Jyoti Singh."

"Age?"

"Twenty."

"Married?" There was a pause.

"She's single," Candice answered.

The nurse glanced up. "Reason for visit?" Jyoti stared straight ahead at nothing. She looked hunted.

"Reason for visit?" the nurse said again.

She drew Candice aside. "Illicit child?" Candice nodded. The woman paused and then said. "Lives with a brother?"

Candice told about Nathan, about Ravi. She described how Jyoti had been brought down from Blackburn after Ravi's mother had died. The woman watched her closely, listening, nodding, scribbling words in a pad.

"And you?" she said after Candice had stopped.

Candice went silent then. "Canadian," she finally mumbled. "I live with them. Teach at the school. She's like a sister."

"It won't be easy," the woman said, almost to herself.

Candice retreated outside and sat with her face to the street, leaning against a cement wall. The three women still on the verandah were wide-bellied, watching her wordlessly.

Eventually Jyoti came out on the arm of the nurse, her skin blenched the colour of milky tea, great pouches of blood ringing her eyes. She slumped to the bench, half conscious. Everyone stared. They'd seen her go in young, strong, and now half an hour later she could barely stand, and reeked unmistakeably of ether.

Jyoti tried to rouse herself. She didn't want to seem ill in front of the women. They would talk, she later told Candice. But the drugs and the trauma were too strong for her. Candice had to carry her to a taxi and lay her down on the back seat to bring her home.

Mid-afternoon sun licked the walls of Candice's room. The mosquito netting swayed and sighed with a steady push of wind. Candice could just make out Jyoti's face through the delicate meshing, pale and brown as a coffee stain against the pillowcase.

Jyoti took days off work. Soon she was eating rice and sitting up to talk. On the third day she gathered all the pillows she could find and ate salted chickpeas in bed, a stack of movie magazines at her elbow. The house resonated once more with sitar and song.

Nathan accepted the illness without complaining or even asking Jyoti what was wrong. He came home early in the afternoons, prepared Ravi's supper and vanished back into town. When he emerged from his bedroom in the morning, his face was puffed and sullen and he smelled of rum. He scowled, but kept his peace. Candice found his lack of prying strange. He probably figured Jyoti had some women's ailment, and left it at that, but the way he had suddenly taken to drink made her uneasy. It was as if he had some private, heavy trouble of his own.

Ravi was being very good. He helped Candice wash his father's shirts, and once she came home to find him sitting in front of a long line of scuff-marked shoes, forearms smeared with black, buffing and shining as if his little life depended on it. Nathan barely noticed. He came in, heated food for the boy and left.

Several days after the operation, Jyoti dressed to return to work. She was still thin, but was looking like her old self. She hummed and sang while she fixed breakfast.

"Why you wearin dat, girl?" Nathan thundered when she put his food down before him. Jyoti shifted nervously in a low-cut fuscia dress. "Me be strong now," she said sweetly.

"To show youself off is why," Nathan screamed. "Strut around so all de men can have a look." Candice stared at him, but his smooth face was flat, expressionless.

In a breathless voice he started to talk about Blackburn. They would go there this weekend for a visit, he said. As he spoke he worked with his fork to debone a small grey fish. His brow was furrowed as if he were fitting together a puzzle.

"Mara will lend me he van," he said studying the skeleton, "an I'll hunt wild fowl like in de olden day." Ravi let out a cheer. Nathan turned to him with eyes red and filmy from drink. "You want to hunt wit me?" he said. "All right. We hunt, man. Candice and Judit, dey fend for demself."

Jyoti stared at her brother. "Blackburn be a nowhere place, man," she said low and sullen, and began to slap dirty dishes one on top of the other.

"You trow my china around like it dirt! I've had it up

to here, girl," Nathan hissed, cutting at his throat with a flat palm. They had forgotten about Candice. She'd never heard them so full of hatred. She was out of her depth. She couldn't say how they had come to this point, or why.

Candice had never seen the Singh house in Blackburn before. It was girded with a hedge of hibiscus that stood taller than a man and bore purple blossoms the size of human faces. Pistils shot out from their centres, scattering dust in the wind. Mrs. Singh was pruning when they arrived in the van.

"Marnin Nathan, marnin," she called, arms and shears waving like an old windmill. She was a squat woman but her limbs were long and slender. Her shirt was cut low, exposing a proud neck and the muscled shoulders of a farmwoman. A beat-up hat veiled her face with shadow.

The estate was meticulous. Candice thought of the disorderly jungle of Nathan's yard in town. Nothing superfluous lay in Mrs. Singh's yard. No children's toys or tools. Pots in the bakehouse gleamed in sunlight. The woodstove's ash was spooned out each evening, the counters scrubbed and polished. Bushes were trimmed flat and square, and flowers had been planted in sharp swatches of colour. Even the laundry flapping in the breeze was arranged with method.

Ravi sprinted over to his grandmother and buried his face in her skirts. Jyoti, pale in a splashy, patterned dress, climbed carefully from the car. Mrs. Singh did not kiss or hug her, she merely nodded as if she were an acquaintance on a busy city street. She led them to the patio where soft drinks and fruit had been laid out. Jyoti sat apart from the rest of the family, quietly sipping a frosted glass.

"Miss Candice," the old woman said. "How you keepin? Me tink you tinner dese days. Natan na feedin you right?"

Nathan scowled when she said this, and after a few minutes, interrupted to announce that he was leaving to hunt. He, his old father, and Ravi disappeared into the green.

The three women sat for a while longer and then decided to take a walk in the rice fields. They followed the trench behind the house single file, Mrs. Singh's splay-toed feet padding softly over ruts from farmers' carts. Mud smooth as soup oozed up between Candice's toes and she marvelled that the old woman's feet remained so pink and dry. Mrs. Singh showed them flocks of tall white birds feeding in the grassy areas beside the trench. These were the birds that Nathan had gone to hunt. He had done it as a boy, she said, and back then they had eaten game almost every week. Now the birds were scarcer, and of course, they had no sons left to do the hunting.

About a half hour later they came to a large tree whose bark had been gouged and slashed by a machete, and hung about it in loose tatters. Mrs. Singh motioned that they should stop. Jyoti slumped down, feverish, Candice noticed, sweating hard, and trying desperately to keep up pretenses. Candice too was tired. She leaned heavily against the enormous flayed trunk.

"It's beautiful here," Candice said, trying to draw the old woman's eyes away from her daughter. "Jyoti's told me stories from her childhood in the fields. She often says she misses it."

The old woman's face darkened. She rubbed a finger along the clean pink of her sole. "Jyoti home be Blackburn now. She never go away no more."

Jyoti didn't flinch. Her eyes blinked just once and then she rose to follow the old woman back to the house. Candice walked behind them, tripping sometimes, clumsy on the rutted donkey path. They knew. They had judged. Jyoti's sentence was Blackburn; she would live out her life tending aging parents until they died, and even then the shame would follow her. Candice felt the force of the girl's fate: brutal, parching as the Guyanese sun that seared her neck, her arms, any skin left exposed as she stumbled behind the women.

At dinner, Candice sat across from Jyoti, but Jyoti refused to look at her. Her eyes were so heavy she couldn't lift them to meet another human face. They were eating a curry made from the birds Nathan caught, birds that had been alive a few hours ago. The meat was so smoky and fresh Candice could barely swallow it. All she could think of were the flocks she'd seen out on the rice fields, rising in a chorus of beating wings above the blistered land.

Xanadu

The boat's name was Xanadu. Her father, Mortimer, had owned in slow succession over the years Xanadu I, Xanadu II, and Xanadu III, three sleek white yachts which he kept moored in the weed-filled basin off the southern rim of Montreal. In the summers he and Jacqueline, her mother, took the boat to the Thousand Islands in Ontario, where the water was wide and much cleaner. This was where she was headed right now, in fact had just about arrived. She eased the car into second and turned down a narrow dirt track beside the marina sign post. The track crossed a field of wild grass and chicory, then plummeted down a tree-lined hill, and Jan saw water.

It was overcast and hot. Jan's legs, in the loose beige shorts stolen from Lenny's cupboard before she left, stuck to the vinyl seat. When she moved, thin streams of sweat, freed from the backs of her knees, dribbled down each calf. She had to peel herself out of the car.

Through all the years of her childhood, Mortimer had dragged his family out to sail. Actually, Jacqueline was quite compliant when it came to Mortimer's hobbies and did not need dragging. She liked the boat and her role as mate, and got busy organizing things. Martha, the youngest daughter, had her own trick. She crawled onto the nearest bunk and fell asleep. Sustained motion did it. Jan had travelled with her many times on planes, in trains and cars, and within minutes of boarding Martha was always heavy-lidded and nodding. Jan, the aloof, eldest child, had no tricks. From the age of ten or eleven she used to hole herself up in the cramped and stuffy bow of the boat and read. This, of course, was a guaranteed ticket to nausea and foul humour as her parents never tired of reminding her. Even now, so many years later, the sight of the glassy lake and the rows of masts made her feel vaguely ill.

"Jan!"

She squinted into the glare, across a closely cropped lawn and a gravel quay. An old man wearing electric blue bermuda shorts and running shoes, his torso naked, was waving at her. Mortimer. For a second she hadn't recognized him. It was true, he was stouter now. The hair on his head had bleached completely white and he had let it grow long to sweep up over the balding areas. He was stiffer, slightly more wooden and hesitant than she remembered, but these, in the end, were small changes.

Jan had spent the last six years in a town in Nova Scotia. She had gone away to college there and dropped out in second year. Her boyfriend, Lenny, ran a café just off campus where she got work as a cook. As a token of love, Lenny changed the café's name to *Jan's Place*, and last winter they put out a book of her recipes, illustrated in pen and ink with peppers and avocados and dancing shivas in the curry section. The years had gone by fast. Faster than she ever would have predicted. Recently, on visits back to Montreal, it was as if everything had shifted very subtly, shifted by a matter of a degree, maybe two, but sufficiently so that things were still familiar, yet somehow not quite recognizable.

"No trouble with the car, or my directions?" Mortimer asked, picking up her bag. She had driven her mother's car from Montreal. She needed it to return to the city to catch an early Sunday flight home. Lenny couldn't last much longer without her. He'd been running the place single-handedly all week and he told her this morning on the phone that he was closing it until she got back.

"Didn't recognize you in the shorts," she said, smiling.

"These?" he said. "My trunks, you mean?" Mortimer always used the word *trunks* instead of bathing suit. It made Jan think of casks of treasure sunk deep beneath the sea. "They're old. Bought them last summer to show Jacqueline I still had some life yet." Mortimer's face changed as he said this, collapsed in on itself like a punctured inner tube. He took Jan's bag and they began walking in the direction of the boats. "The place is deserted," he said. "There's not a breath of wind. I've never seen it so still."

Water stretched out before them like an immense sheet of glass. Boats sat immobile in their slots, their masts poking up like needles. The sky was silver, so bright and uniform that Jan could not look at it straight on. There seemed no clear division between it and the watery horizon.

She followed him down, across the lawn, over a marshy spot with a makeshift plank bridge to the wharf. Mortimer's weight made the wharf creak and sway, and she slowed down, feeling old, familiar sensations of being on water. Mid-way down the dock a man about her age was on his knees, scrubbing the side of a boat. His skin was the rich colour of coffee and he half turned but did not say hello. Just beyond him on an older, scuff-marked boat with the name *Rednose* stamped on her stern, two other men sat under a canopy playing cards. Mortimer waved and they stopped their game to squint at Jan.

They would have seen Martha already. Martha was

dark, like Mortimer had been, short like him and delicate. Jan was tall, light-haired, thicker-set. She had Jacqueline's eyes, steel grey, spaced like a cat's. Both she and Martha looked young, far too young to be offspring of the old man in the crazy shorts. Mortimer had been well into his forties when Jan was conceived and Jan's earliest memories of her father were of someone old. When he took her out in her pram people thought he was a grandfather. Mortimer had always been the parent who needed attention, lots of care. Jan remembered a family story of herself at five announcing that when she grew up she'd be a doctor, to look after him in his old age.

When she was still quite small, seven or so, she went through a phase where she would imagine his death. She remembered one night at a rented cottage in the Laurentians. It was summer and she was lying with all the covers kicked off on a cot beside Martha's bed. The room was small and the sisters had dragged the cot close so they could whisper. Jan was lying there thinking about Mortimer, and all of a sudden sadness came up out of nowhere, like waves do on the ocean. It was the image of Mortimer alone, hating the aloneness, maybe even afraid, and way beyond their reach that made her cry. She sobbed hard for a long time that night, alarming Martha, but she didn't know what it was, couldn't find words to explain. All she said was, "He could die, you know. Father could die."

In the boat's cockpit, Martha was lying perfectly still, the oval of her face turned upwards, as if for a kiss. Jan wondered if she remembered that night, the first time either of them had sensed the finality, the first time she'd mourned. It was all fictional, of course. In the end no one died and there was no reason to get worked up. Mortimer had lived on, fought and quarrelled with all his paternal vigour for two succeeding decades.

Everyone in their family lived for ages. Jacqueline's parents were still going strong, the aunts and uncles were all healthy. Mortimer's parents were dead, but they had died years ago, before Jan could talk or form memories, so they didn't count. Jan and Martha grew up remarkably death-free. That was why this one still hadn't sunken in. It was so novel. It also came from the wrong corner. Mortimer was still alive and kicking; it was Jacqueline, strong, health-conscious Jacqueline, just turned fifty-five, who had gone down. Nobody could quite believe it.

"Jan," Martha said, opening her eyes. "You made it. Mortimer was threatening to push me in and make me tow all by myself."

That was Martha. She always knew the things to say to make Mortimer laugh, to loosen up the mood. She was tanned a deep brown and her teeth flashed like the froth of waves. She had just returned from Spain where she was studying languages. Mortimer stood on the dock, smiling at the image Martha conjured up.

It was their first free time together since the funeral. For three weeks now, Mortimer's friends had come around, taken them for meals, for coffee, come to the house to chat. That had been exhausting, but good in a way, because it kept them all busy in the first days of shock. Mortimer wept a lot in the beginning. He looked awful, like he wasn't sleeping, and in the middle of conversations his face went ashen and limp. The last two or three days had been better. He was speaking more, acting his old self. Neither Jan nor Martha had cried yet. Jan knew that if it had been Mortimer in the coffin she would have gone wild with grief, wept whole days without shame. Not because she loved him more, or loved Jacqueline any less, but because with Jacqueline death was different. Jacqueline had wide, veiny hands. Her nails were short, often with a thin line of dirt near the cuticle from all the gardening she did. Jacqueline would be fine in the earth. It wouldn't frighten her. Mortimer, on the other hand, would be inconsolable. He would hammer at the coffin until his fists were bloody and raw, scream until he was hoarse. Jan went crazy imagining it.

Jan wasn't sure about this trip to the boat. She thought it would stir up all the grief again. But Mortimer said he wanted to get out of the city, it was time to get the wind in his sails again. Besides, the girls had never seen Xanadu III. It was a foot longer than the last one and even faster.

Jacqueline had died here. The way Mortimer told it, she felt ill in the afternoon and complained of a headache after a long and gusty day of sailing. In the middle of the night she sat bolt upright and shouted out obscenities. Mortimer didn't tell this part immediately. He was shy to admit that his wife's last words were angry, dirty things, flung out in her bewilderment. The autopsy showed a blood clot to the brain and a massive haemorrhage, as if a bomb had exploded inside the skull.

"Climb aboard," Mortimer said and swung himself up over the wire railing. He went forward to open the front hatch and make sure the anchor and all the lines were in order. Jan climbed into the cockpit and sat down beside her sister. They smiled at each other almost guiltily and then turned to stare at the glassy water.

"He's so up," Jan said.

"Yeah," said Martha, screwing her eyes in the glare. "He's still swinging."

"What'll happen when we go, Martha?"

A whistled refrain came from below. Jan cocked her head. "Remember that?" She began to sing.

What shall we do with the drunken sailor,
What shall we do with the drunken sailor,
What shall we do with the drunken sailor,
Ear-lie in the morning?

Mortimer had taught it to them. It was an old drinking song, and Jan had always felt extremely sad about the sailor who was thrown into the scuppers, doused with sea water and finally keel-hauled, all for taking a drink. When she was young and Mortimer got sullen from too much scotch, the rhyme and its atrocities would come to her.

"I'm staying," Martha said.

Jan looked at her. She had offered first, as effortlessly as breathing. Martha the martyr, Jan thought, feeling mean and small even as she formed the words. She always did things right. Jan wasn't generous enough by half, she somehow lacked the instincts to tend to her father.

"What the hell. I can't live in Barcelona forever."

"But you're almost through," Jan said, thinking of the degree. Martha would have a master's if she finished in Spain, like Mortimer, who had one from Boston. "You can't give that up. He wouldn't want it."

"I'd die to think he was alone," she said and raised her eyebrows because Mortimer was coming back towards the cockpit.

Mortimer took them a long way out, nearly an hour's motor away. The boat sliced easily through the heat and the water, which was turquoise, almost like sea, except that there wasn't a wave around. Lower down the St. Lawrence, near Montreal, the water was black and foul-smelling. Mortimer kept his boat there in the off season, and spent weekends floating on urban waste.

He turned into a small bay where half a dozen boats were bobbing lazily. They resembled birds, swans or marsh cranes, feeding in a sheltered corner. Mortimer cut the engine. "Well, go on," he shouted at Jan, who was perched on the roof of the cabin, daydreaming and staring at a picnic party on a neighbouring yacht. His voice hung nakedly in the hushed noon air. "We'll drift right into them if you don't get to it!"

Jan jumped towards the bow and began to fumble with the coil of rope for the anchor. She wasn't used to this. It had been Jacqueline's job. Jacqueline lowered anchors and bumpers, raised sails, took them down again, folded, stored them. Year after year she packed lunches, unpacked them, found the plates and things to serve them on, gathered up the garbage, mopped up spills. Jacqueline alone knew how to flush the little chemical toilet hidden in one corner of the bow. She never shared her knowledge, never delegated.

She got the anchor down, and Mortimer smiled at her. She knew at base she was very much like her mother, sturdy, strong, unafraid. She did not mind the tilt of boats in a high wind, had capsized smaller boats and righted herself many times when she was young. She loved to dive off the stern and could swim kilometres without tiring. She didn't know what Mortimer would do with the boat now that Jacqueline was gone. He couldn't manage it himself, that much was certain. His balance was bad. Each time he moved up along the decks Jan drew in her breath and said prayers.

They decided to swim before lunch. The wind was beginning to pick up but the air was heavy and very hot. Jan moved through the water as easily as the pale, sleek boats owned by her father. She loved the gliding feeling when she built up speed and a steady rhythm. Waves nudged her and rolled off her back into a streaming wake. She and Martha swam far out, side by side, towards the next yacht.

"We should go back," Martha yelled to her. "Swim with Mortimer."

They were with the wind and came up to the boat in no time. There was no sign of him. Jan's chest went tight as she scanned the water's surface. She heard Martha's voice, small, terrified, calling his name. "Oh," Martha gasped. "It's okay. He's here."

Jan passed behind the stern to the other side. The ashy taste of fear filled her mouth. Mortimer was treading water almost underneath the hull. He was in trouble. He kept flailing one arm up, causing his face to submerge in the gentle roll of waves.

Then she saw the pink shape in his hand. A sponge.

She and Martha raced towards him. "Here, Mortimer, let us." A thin film had grown at the boat's waterline and he was trying to scrub it off. Mortimer jabbed at the stains a few times and then handed her the sponge. She took it without a break in her stroke, like a relay runner receiving a baton. The easiest way to do it was to drag the sponge along the boat's side with her left hand while the right swung in broad, freestyle strokes. She did the circumference while Martha helped Mortimer back onto the boat to get lunch.

Lunch was an uncomplicated affair of potato salad, bought at a Montreal deli, smoked meat and beer. Martha, who had been relegated to the position of cook, stuck her head out of the cabin at one point and said they'd forgotten plates. Mortimer laughed and told them they'd have to eat out of containers like he used to do in his bachelor days. Jan licked at peppercorns embedded in a string of bluish fat on her meat and thought of Jacqueline. She would have brought fruit, leaf salad, something raw and fresh. Jacqueline would have hated this meal.

Wind was teasing the river, goading its surface into small, lapping waves. Mortimer started the engine and set his daughters to work. He stood at a thin rimmed wheel shouting orders. Jan took the huge frontsail out of a bag. It had been meticulously pleated and stowed and it struck her that the last person to touch it was probably her mother. She partially unfurled it and attached the clips to the front stay. Martha, meanwhile, was fastening sheets and readying everything for hoisting. They tried to pull the anchor, but it seemed to have stuck on something. Jan had to tug and tug, and finally it came ripping through the blue-green in an explosion of mud and weed. Great clots of brown stuck to it and Martha dirtied her shirt, her shoe, and tracked it back to the cockpit. Jan was left to do the sails.

The engine droned and the deck beneath her feet began to vibrate. She felt the boat swing around. Mortimer yelled that she could pull any time, and all at once she was surrounded by slapping sail, huge, shining, blown loudly by the wind. It was like standing between the legs of giants, or in the middle of a storm. Xanadu lurched to the right, her winches screaming as the sails pulled tight. The boat began to heel and suddenly there was silence. Jan clung to the guard rail, listening to the trapped silence of wind embraced by sail.

They sailed long into the afternoon. Mortimer was so pleased to have wind, so happy to be out on his boat again, that he became daring and insisted on forging further and further on. The sun glared down from a strange whitish sky making

Jan think of naked lightbulbs.

Towards four o'clock the sky suddenly seemed to slip. It wasn't a momentous change by any means, and Jan wasn't sure at first that anything had happened. The clouds were still luminous and hazy, but there was something threatening in the way they now hung over the water. Mortimer continued their course. He didn't say a thing, but his eyes narrowed and he watched with concentration. Then, without explanation, he told Jan to lower the sails.

Their silence was masked by engine sounds. Mortimer had turned the boat around and was racing dark and heavy clouds gathering behind them. Jan sat with her feet braced against the opposite seat, watching a spider. It was trying to climb the slippery, sheer white surface and kept tumbling back to its starting point. She didn't want to kill it. Spiders got rid of flies, and besides, Jacqueline once told her that killing one meant rain. Slowly, without knowing how long she'd been listening to it, Jan realized the motor was sounding different. Mortimer shifted into high gear and it strained loudly, but they were barely moving. He began fiddling with the lever, pushing it into reverse, then forward again, but still the boat wouldn't budge. "Damn," he said. Drops of water had begun to fall, heavy drops, but intermittently. He cut the engine. The antenna at the top of the mast buzzed like an angry insect.

Jan felt suddenly tired. Her stomach was queasy from the heavy lunch and the constant rocking of the boat. She had no more patience for the water and began to wish urgently for land. Mortimer removed his shoes. "Propellor's jammed," he said, and before they really understood, he let down the ladder and was in the water.

She and Martha hung over the side, watching. Martha

was ripping at the buttons of her shirt. "He shouldn't," she began. Waves knocked Mortimer close to the hull. He clung to the ladder, which shifted with the rocking of the boat, scraping against its side. Jan couldn't speak. She hated seeing him helpless. She should be down there, not him. Lightning might strike. He could drown. Mortimer gulped at the air and disappeared beneath the roiling blackish waters.

The rain grew steadier, soundlessly marking the water in intricate welted spheres. The boat rocked and drifted closer to the shoreline. Seconds went by and Mortimer didn't reappear. "We shouldn't have let him," Martha said. She was in her shorts and bathing suit top and began to cry. Jan watched her. It was all happening so fast and yet so unutterably slowly. Her brain was no help. She kept imagining she saw his face, bloated, ghostly, resurfacing on the water. She made silent, half-coherent pacts with herself. She would move home. She'd never, ever fight with him again. She'd go back to school, leave the café, leave Lenny, anything if only he were safe.

There was a splash and Mortimer emerged, fists full of long green weed. Waves slapped the side of the boat and rebounded, tossing him away. Jan couldn't move. She wanted to call him, to scream, but her voice failed, she couldn't get the sounds out. Martha was waving, sobbing but the wind was too strong and Mortimer didn't hear her. He dove again, disappearing below the dark, tossing surface.

A spot of blue appeared below the waves, shimmering and glowing in the muted light. Mortimer's shorts, Jan realized. They were barely recognizable, transformed by water into something eerily beautiful. He emerged just as she was thinking this, spluttering, moving his head, waving a fresh handful of weed. He had dislodged great chunks of it. Long, hairlike strands were streaming out behind the boat, only to be sucked down seconds later and disappear into the swirling eddies. Mortimer climbed onto the deck, his torso draped in green, and Martha handed him a towel. She and Jan were suddenly like children, reverent, closely watching. He started the motor, and the boat moved forward as if a giant hand had reached down and pushed.

"You did it," Martha cried out, laughing, and hugged him hard.

The rain was coming faster and behind them, a stick of lightning fell through the sky. Mortimer's hair stood upright from the static, making him look dishevelled, odd, like a shipwrecked hero. Jan loved him at that instant, and in later years would return to it again and again, Mortimer staring out at the horizon, rain falling all about him, a proud old man in a pair of unexpected, electric blue shorts, guiding them back to shore.

Remembering the Dead

Maude sits alone, completely clothed in black and sipping wine. The wine is white. Warm and sour going down. Warm as summer, making her head light and swimmy.

She sits on a deserted terrace, elbows on cold marble. It's November although you'd never know it. A pale sun washes the streets. It has been so soft this year, caressing, lulling her. Her favourite season in Montreal. Usually filled with violent shifts, strong winds. This one so gentle, golden all through October, November.

A group of people are standing in a park underneath a bronze angel. The angel hovers above a soldier, green hand upon his cheek. A great amplified voice says, 'For those who have died'. The words are caught up by the wind and brought to Maude across the empty terrace. A microphone squeals and Maude thinks of death. So many boys died far from home, the voice says, left to rot in fields of clay.

Ceux qui sont morts. Death in two tongues. All tongues go suddenly still, heads bow. From where she sits, Maude can see stains of red on their lapels. Bleeding hearts. As if the pins holding their poppies had pierced right through.

Two figures stand wiping at their eyes. Two mothers weeping. Old, white-haired. They look on beside rows of men in uniforms, stiff, reverential in the thin November light. The drums start like drops of rain. They build slowly, filling the street until the noise is huge, like gunfire. The men's feet start. Someone shouts and the cadets surge forward in one body lifting hard black boots. Rat-a-tat. Girls in dark green, arms swinging, hips bulging, march stiff as dolls, as wooden puppets. They are so ugly, faces long, breasts and buttocks bursting the seams of their men's clothing.

Around the statue they march, past the terrace. The crowd breaks up, drifts off now to march with the cadets. Old ones with ribbons, badges, knees up, chests out, bleary-eyed, still keeping time. They push their faces forward. Chins up, stern. Rigid limbs. Rat-a-tat. Limbs in time. Rat-a-tat.

The two old women follow. One hides her face in a dark veil. Her legs are like the legs of a bird. Thin and brittle. Snap like twigs when you get that old. She looks at Maude and whispers. *Chuchotement.* A dried leaf flies up and hits Maude in the cheek. She jumps flailing all alone out on the terrace. The women stare and frown and Maude sits again, sheepish, and pulls her glass towards her over the smooth stone table top.

"Maude!"

Bob, his hair white and streaming, is half running towards her across the street. He is dragging someone by the elbow. A big man with yellowish hair. *Merde.* He always brings his friends, beer-swigging with all their opinions.

"You're all in black," Bob says, breathing hard. "Remembering the dead?" The two men laugh.

He is right. She is all in black. Maude thinks of black panties that Bob cannot possibly see. Black stockings, black jeans, dark boots, a black sweater that swamps her small frame. No bra. Her face is pale as a moon ringed with a rust halo of hair.

He doesn't kiss her but as he sits down, reaches under the table. Warm hand on her thigh. He smiles, eyes shifting quickly from her, and introduces the friend.

Arnold has greased hair the colour of a car's headlights: white with yellow streaks. Stained fingers and teeth, small filmy irises. He is a columnist for an English newspaper, and might be in his sixties. He lights a cigarette and even before it burns down is lighting another.

Maude is glad they are on a terrace. The smoke drifts aimlessly and spills onto the street. Their words scatter with the smoke. Scatter like so much seed, or dust. She must not think of it. Her breasts are swollen, full and ripe.

"The mayor's too old now," Bob says. "It's just as well he's stepping down. A bent old man. Have you seen him lately?"

Arnold nods his great streaked head. "Twenty-nine years in office," he says. "Long time for anyone. I bet that's more years than you've been alive," he says to Maude.

"Keep talking and you'll lose me a girlfriend, Bob says and laughs his big, man's laugh. "She's our side of thirty."

Maude sips her wine and tilts her head back into the sun. Orange globes swirl on her eyelids and summer slips deep down inside of her. First mouth, then throat, then belly. Bellyful of warmth. If she kept it, she'd swear off drink, swear off bars and blustering men breathing smoke.

More beers. Bob's colour rises. He's a Scot who loves his scotch. "He's a drunk," Bob says. "Spineless too. Shifts like a weathervane. Christ, you breathe and the man changes direction."

Careless talk. Maude doesn't know who they're attacking. Arnold tosses his head, his long teeth grinding peanuts.

Bob loves to talk. When liquor's in his blood he has no shame. He'll say anything. It cost him his marriage. A job. When they first met, months ago, it had thrilled her. Now she knows it's not him, not courage, just drink.

Bob speaks French when he's drunk. It forks his tongue and turns him loose and wild. He loves women. All French except for the wife who was a Scot like him, and a lousy cook. But the mistresses are French. Bob the hedonist. French women, French food. He loves and eats.

His family is grown now. The children are scattered here and there. English kids are like that. Catch onto any wind that blows through the city; touch down in Toronto, New York, wherever. That's where they are. The wife and her youngest are in Toronto, the eldest is an actor in New York. Maude has never met them. She just hears their voices when they call, and she's seen photographs of children posing in a park.

Bob never speaks about his children. Once he said he should have stayed single.

"Montreal's an old whore," Arnold says. A speck of nut flies from his lip onto the table. "A warm old whore that everyone loves. No matter who runs her she'll always be the same."

"What would you know about whores?" Bob says, laughing.

Maude breathes. Her breasts shift slightly, heavy on her chest. She has never felt so full. She thinks of seed pods, milkweed pushing to burst. Brown husks with white spidery fibres inside. Silk hiding seed, exploding in the fields. She wants to see it grow, this fullness in her belly.

"The city runs itself," Arnold says, and wipes froth from his fine lip hairs. "Has for years," he continues. "Men just like to flatter themselves they have a say."

Maude's eyes meet Arnold's. His words are wise. Too bad about his looks.

"Take this so-called new government," Arnold says. "New men with so-called new ideas. Just watch and see in ten years if anything has changed."

But things do change! Maude thinks. They do. She never would have thought she'd feel it so strongly. Before, when she was young, she'd loved carelessly, so many men. And once before, when she was twenty, this thing had happened. It had been in summer with that boy Germain. When she'd told him he had cried and cried, spilling tears. She'd had to hold him one entire night. She'd been strong then, and determined. Then it was nothing. She hadn't wanted it. Simple as burning off a wart.

"Hey," Bob says to her. "You still there? You still with us?"

Maude nods and stares at her black lap. She is thirty-three now. Thirteen years since the last time. Unlucky. Strange how this would pain her. She could feel it already. Like ripping out part of herself. Killing herself. Bob wouldn't cry. No, he wouldn't even want to know.

The sun is dropping. Long shadows fall across the street, striping it in black. A mess of bottles clutters the table. Saucers spill ash and broken butts. Bob tries to light a cigarette in the wind. Fails.

"Geez," Bob says. "Can't even light a goddamn cigarette." He's drunk. "It's late," he says. "Let's go." He puts dollars under a saucer and Arnold slips a large bill under a glass. They get up unsteadily and navigate through the tables, Bob clutching at the backs of chairs. Maude follows him. He's an athletic man and by the time they reach the street, is walking fine.

"Hey you," Bob says, slipping his arm around her shoulders. "You're a beauty when you're glum." Arnold looks away. They walk up the middle of a deserted street, three abreast, little Maude all in black, flanked by two tall, white-haired men.

At an intersection, they stop. All three together, as if choreographed. There are no cars, but they are creatures of the city, creatures of habit. Maude looks down into a sewer. In the garbage and the leaves a fleck of red catches her eye. It's a poppy stuck in the grating, its pin and centre fallen off. Bright bloom in the fading light.

Prosperity

It was always blowing here. The house was near the beach where the ocean sent waves arcing wildly. Wind tore in from the open water, across flat sands and marshes, unable to slow before it reached the trees and bushes at the roadside, slapping up against barn doors and cottages like this one built just a couple of miles in from the shore.

Jackie came into the dining-room cradling a ceramic pot. She stopped in the doorway. "My God, it's a wonder the whole house doesn't blow down."

"What's that rhyme?" She stepped lightly over to the stroller parked in a corner and peered in. "I'll huff and I'll puff," she said, scrunching her eyes and pulling a wide grin, "and I'll blo-ow your house down."

"Mother," Casey said. "You'll twist his mind. Why do people insist on telling babies about wolves eating pigs?"

"He doesn't talk yet," Jackie answered haughtily. "Besides, I didn't even mention the wolf." She turned her attention to Casey's husband. "John, you have to eat some of this." She held out the pot.

John looked dubiously at his mother-in-law. It was Rosh Hashanah, the Jewish New Year, and he wasn't familiar with Jewish customs. John and Casey lived in Toronto and this was their first autumn visit to New Brunswick. In her own home,

Casey did her best to ignore the high holidays. She and John didn't practise any form of religion, really, except a rather non-committal exchange of gifts at Christmas. John took the pot from his mother-in-law and lifted the lid. Threads of something like treacle trailed from the cover. "Honey," he said, sniffing.

Jackie laughed. He looked as if he'd expected something exotic, something hinting of mystery. She nodded at the centerpiece of gleaming fruit. "You have to eat apples dipped in honey at the start of every year. It's the Jewish charm for prosperity."

They were an odd family. One of the early mixed marriages where neither partner imposed his denominational will on the other. Jackie was Anglican. In her younger days, a svelte blonde with sculpted, nordic features. Sid, on the other hand, was from an orthodox family. One of his cousins was a Hasid. In his twenties, during a rather out of character phase of rebellion, he'd scandalized his family and the local Jewish community by taking a gentile girl as his bride. Jackie, who found Sid every bit as exotic as he found her, was willing, but she too had a headstrong, rebellious side. She refused to convert, even though by her own admission Christianity meant very little to her.

Sid insisted his daughters be raised as Jews, but then never seemed to have the time or interest to oversee their training. The task fell inevitably, as most mundane tasks did—like walking the dog or cleaning up after supper—to his wife. Jackie set about learning Jewish lore with the zeal of an amateur anthropologist. She memorized prayers for light and wine, hunted down recipes from the Middle East. Her upper crust English was peppered with Yiddish idiom. She gave dissertations on Judaism to anyone who would listen.

John took an apple, already peeled and cored by Jackie, and put it on his plate. He dribbled honey over it. "Like this?" he said, popping it in his mouth. "Anyone else want some prosperity?"

Casey took a slice of fruit from her husband but Glenda, the eldest, just grimaced. She was remembering Rosh Hashanah dinner a year ago. Glenda lived in Moncton not far from Sid and Jackie, and unlike her sister she made the pilgrimage to their cottage every fall. Last year, Jaime had been with her. The man she'd loved for almost five years.

She hadn't seen him in weeks. Not since the night she went by to pick up files and the last of her clothes. He'd kept the house. It was in his name, bought with his money. And she'd been very generous about their possessions, taking only what was necessary. It made her too sad, rummaging through the kitchen for pots and plates, choosing plants and records and some of the art work she felt she couldn't live without. Most of it she left for him. The walls of her new place were bare; the waxed pine floors shone nakedly, unencumbered. The whole thing matched her spirit, light and empty, refusing to clutter itself with the baggage of old lives left behind.

Glenda was a doctor. She worked occasionally at the hospital, but mostly she took visits at her office or made house calls. She was pretty content with her life. She prided herself on being a people's doctor: a woman who took the time to chat with patients and play with the children she examined. Hers wasn't a sophisticated practice. She did no research, published no papers. It was simple, small time medicine and it suited her just fine.

Jaime was the opposite. He was a psychiatrist with a specialty in split personality. He worked in a ward and had already published a number of papers on the biochemical underpinnings of the disease. His mind was always restless, forever digging. Glenda felt like a featherweight next to him. In her family she'd always been the smart one, the achiever, but next to Jaime it seemed she had no intellect at all.

She'd gone blithely along with their life, trying to believe they were happy, trying to believe it was fine, even though Jaime was so dark sometimes, and difficult to sound. He never spoke just for the pleasure of letting words flow. He was always measured, editing, holding back. He didn't praise or speak of love, and Glenda, whose nature was soft and pliant, withered slightly, turned inward and unsure.

One morning in mid-summer she was called out on a home visit. The day was bright and she decided on an impulse to walk. The quickest route took her across the campus of Moncton's university. Kids in T-shirts lounged on stairs and played frisbee on the grass. A few were dozing in the shade, trying to read. There was a lazy, holiday feel to the day and it made her slow her pace, look about as she walked. She turned down a street off the campus and passed a café with a wide front window. It had just been cleaned and an image of herself, womanly, pale, with her hair piled in a loose bun, smiled out expectantly. She liked the way she looked in that moment, took the time to savour it. Hers was no longer a girlish beauty. She could remember being a student as if it were yesterday, but whenever she walked across campus, people looked so young. The boys especially seemed like teenagers with their bony limbs and deliberately careless dress. She was thirty-two, her features rounded and smoothed, and she felt good. She was wearing fuscia, her best colour; bright bloom on this summer day. The vision of herself, smiling in the glass, would later return to Glenda with painful clarity. She'd see it as a snapshot, an image frozen, sloughed off from the flux of time.

As she looked through the smoky surface to the café's interior she caught sight of Jaime, sitting at a side table. She thought at first she must be wrong. What would he be doing here, so far from the hospital in the middle of a weekday morning? She squinted into the light. It was him. There was no mistaking the dark head, the shoulders at once broad and sloping. He was engrossed in discussion with someone she'd never seen before. The woman across from him was listening, hunched towards him, her eyes locked with his.

Glenda went up to the window and rapped her knuckles until it shook. It was like a silent film, theatre in mime. She saw without hearing. People were talking, laughing, lifting things to their mouths. Then, almost in unison, they turned to stare. The place was full of students and it seemed to Glenda they watched her as if she were crazy, with a kind of mock indifference. Jaime was looking at her, slack-mouthed, but she kept hitting the glass with her hand. Eventually he came outside. The woman didn't follow. When Glenda turned to the table where they'd been sitting the seats were empty. She'd vanished, leaving no trace.

A year ago, Jaime had been with her. He'd sat here in the very seat where John now sat, an apple in the middle of his plate, Jackie hovering over him with Talmudic explanations. Glenda got up and went to look at the baby. Wind was rattling the picture window in the living-room and the infant turned to the sound with solemn, worried eyes. He smiled when he saw Glenda, his whole face opening. She smiled back, offering her smallest finger.

Jackie came up beside her. "His first Rosh Hashanah," she said, bending over the carriage. Benjamin, who was lying on his back, stared up neutrally. "It's a blessing to have new life in the house." She bent lower and kissed the child. In a melodious voice she crooned, "You'll come back next year too, when you're on your feet. Every autumn at Granny's house with the wind blowing off the beach and everyone inside all cozy and warm."

In the clear, grey eyes of her nephew Glenda saw years stretch before her. This child had somehow bumped her over the line. She was no longer young. She'd be thirty-three this winter. It was something she didn't like to think about. She felt like a girl still, capable of any one of many destinies. She still talked of going overseas, a dream she'd had for years. She'd move to some African country, set up practice for a year or two. Or maybe she could take a sabbatical at home and try her hand at pottery. She'd had quite a talent when she was in school. Recently, these plans had begun to ring a little hollow. She couldn't turn to them without nagging thoughts of her age, of the years already gone. Her life was settled now. No matter how she looked at it, there were constants, patterns. Her small town practice, the quiet, east coast life with a string of relationships that never seemed to come together, this was Glenda. The chances of her breaking off into something fresh dimmed with passing seasons.

She knew other women doctors, still single like herself, meting out time in the examining room. Somehow they seemed younger than the wives who crowded their offices with endless strings of toddlers. They were less encumbered, free. No loads of laundry soaking in their sinks, no meals to fix at night. You might see them strolling on a Saturday, window shopping as though they had all the time in the world. And then one day, when they reached forty or so, it changed. She'd seen it happen again and again, but never allowed it might be her fate. They became spinsters, and you got the sense they'd always remain solitary. It was as if they'd cheated Nature, leapt from girlhood directly to middle age, skirting the rich, complex ground of woman's life that lay between.

Jackie announced that dinner was ready. She brought a metal platter laden with brisket and vegetables into the room and everyone was seated. Jackie pulled the carriage close to the table. She left her plate almost untouched, performing a monologue for the child, explaining how it never made sense to her that the year should start in the dead of winter, when everything was cold and buried in snow. The Jews were right, she said. The new year started in autumn after the vacations ended. Casey caught Glenda's eye conspiratorily. Jackie had found the perfect audience.

Glenda toyed with food that was no longer warm. It was as if the universe had shifted at some quiet moment while her attention had been elsewhere. She'd lost her place. Her orbit had been broken. The other planets circled slowly, confidently in familiar grooves, but she'd wobbled off track. She was drifting without meaning or direction.

The baby began to cry. He was worn out from the attention, wanting food and sleep. Casey took him in her arms, mock waltzing, but he screamed harder. Everybody stopped talking to watch.

"Take him upstairs," John said. His voice was calm and Glenda saw how it was with them. Somehow their lives had blended. No need for drawn-out talks. Casey headed for the bedroom. The wails eventually subsided and John got up and went to look in on them. Glenda and her parents were left in the living-room, listening to wind trapped inside the chimney.

"You remember what it was like," Jackie said to Sid. "The crying and the feeding, night after night. It was so simple then."

When Glenda left, it was almost eleven. She had a busy day coming up. It made her tired even to think of it. Really she should take the day off. It was one of the most important holidays of the year. But to be Jewish in Moncton, especially the way Glenda was Jewish, coming from a mixed family, carried little weight. Glenda's colleagues didn't think of her as any different from themselves, and for her the New Year meant simply a pleasant dinner with Jackie and Sid and bouts of drowsiness the next morning. That was the extent of her observance.

The wind was like a wall around the house. She walked, head bent as if in prayer, to her car. Wind threw her hair against her cheek, blowing it into her mouth and eyes as she struggled with the car's lock. Finally she was inside, the interior lit up like a candle. She slammed the door shut and then had to open it again to fit the key into the ignition.

The road was almost completely black. Every quarter mile or so a streetlamp appeared shrouded in a faint halo of light, but as soon as she passed it the night swallowed her up again. Her eyes followed the broken line snaking out in front of her. She was floating. Disembodied in a place where space and time had no meaning. An image of Jaime rose before her. She saw the deep judging eyes lined from fatigue and work, the mouth curling into his half-smile. Wind brushed against her car. The trees lining the road were a dark blur, keening and swaying, and great clots of cloud rushed overhead obscuring the moon.

She reached for the radio, thinking it would anchor her, give her something solid in the surrealistic sweep of night, but static filled the car's cabin. She was too far from the city to pick up her usual station. She fiddled with the knob, trying to find something with a beat, rock and roll, even disco. Before she could grasp what was happening, a dark form leapt out in front of her, jolting the car sidelong towards the ditch. All she saw was the jump of pale flank, eyes like planets flickering in the night. Then it was gone and she was fighting for control, the car careening madly, her foot jamming the brakes. She screamed to a stop and got out, shaking so hard she could hear the clattering of teeth. Wind swiped at her scarf, flinging it from her neck onto the asphalt and spiriting it away. The fender was bent in like an accordion. She brushed her hand against it and felt something sticky and warm. In the yellow beams of headlight she saw that she was smeared with blood.

"Oh my God," Glenda said aloud. Her voice was small and hoarse, but it reassured her. "Oh my God," she said again. She knew now it was a deer, gone crazy with the lights, which had jumped into the road. Judging by the damage to her car it was hit badly, but at least it had the strength to run off. Maybe it was all right.

She climbed into the car, did a full turn and limped slowly back in the direction from which she'd come. The car was smoking when she reached the path to her father's cottage. She inched her way along, finally making it into the yard. Sid came out onto the balcony in his bathrobe and slippers. Then he was beside her, taking her in his arms, supporting her beside the steaming, battered car. She started to cry, feebly at first, as if she couldn't find her voice, then louder until she was wailing like a child. Her father's arms were stiff, hesitant, but still she couldn't find the strength to stop.

Later that night, after phone calls to the police, after the game-warden had been alerted, a search party sent out and the deer found and shot, Glenda sat in her parents' dining-room, scotch glass in hand, surrounded by a weary, anxious audience of family. Her voice rang strangely young in her ears, like that of a child awakened from sleep, recounting night terrors. She described the car beetling along the unlit road, the headlights barely denting the gloom. She tuned in to a rock station. She could even remember the song. A Van Morrison number she'd danced to years ago in high school.

"Everything before the deer is so vivid," she said. "Vivid and slow, like in a film."

She was thinking of Jaime, but this part she didn't tell. Jaime rising before her so clearly she could have lifted her hand from the steering wheel and touched him. He hovered silent and heavy, filling the car with his presence.

She told about the animal leaping out of nowhere. The film reel spun crazily then. She had an indistinct recollection of white flank and eyes, cold flames in the night. It was like a dream, wavering for several seconds, then sucked back into darkness. The next thing she knew the car was swerving, skidding along the asphalt and she hit the shoulder.

Jackie looked exhausted with her hair down and her face stripped of make-up. She watched Glenda closely, checking for signs of shock or other more subtle damage.

"Oh baby," she said. "After all you've been through."

Sid told her to go to sleep. They'd phone her office first thing next morning and tell them she was sick.

"Sure," said Jackie. "Stay. We'll take a quiet day together, just the family."

Jackie reached to refill her daughter's glass but Glenda shook her head and took instead a slice of fruit from a plate on the kitchen table. It was the centrepiece of apples left over from dinner. Jackie had covered it with cellophane but the flesh of most of the fruit had oxidized. Brown fuzz spread in uneven patches along the surfaces. Glenda dribbled honey over the piece she had selected, drowning the rusty spots with gold.

No one said a word as she lifted the whole thing to her mouth and swallowed it quickly down.